A LETHAL LADY!

Gabe loped his gelding over to the fallen woman and dismounted to kneel by her side. He gripped her shoulder and started to turn her over but, suddenly, she screamed and thrust a small kitchen knife at his belly. Long Rider just managed to twist his shoulders enough so that the knife only cut a mean gash across the hard muscles of his belly instead of ripping into his vitals.

She stabbed again . . .

LONG RIDER

THE BUFFALO HUNTERS

CLAY DAWSON

10

CHARTER BOOKS, NEW YORK

THE BUFFALO HUNTERS

A Charter Book/published by arrangement with
the author

PRINTING HISTORY
Charter Original/May 1990

ISBN: 1-55773-335-X

PRINTED IN THE UNITED STATES OF AMERICA

10 9 8 7 6 5 4 3 2 1

CHAPTER ONE

Long Rider eased his lank frame up in his stirrups as his gray eyes tracked across the rolling landscape of central Wyoming. He had ridden up from the Big Horn Mountains just to see the hills covered with buffalo grass and bright spring flowers. His favorite flower was the purplish, furry-petaled mayflower, though he reckoned that the white-and-pink primrose ran a mighty close second. There were also yellow and purple violets, buttercups, and blazing stars flourishing in the shade of rocks and ravines. Only a fool would ever starve in this country, even without weapons, because chokecherries, wild plums, gooseberries, and currant thickets were easy to find near the streambeds. Long Rider's favorite was the wild buffalo berry that filled the many draws and ravines.

There were folks who probably thought a man riding alone in this country with nothing better to do than sightsee was slightly touched in the head, but Gabe Conrad was not one who cared what anyone thought. He simply did what he wanted to do and the hell with convention. Unlike most men, Gabe had a sense that the wide-open freedom of this country was rapidly being trampled by too many men, regulations, and fences.

Hell, he thought, a man has to go damn near to Montana country anymore just to catch a glimpse of a buffalo.

Gabe relaxed and spurred his horse into an easy gallop, thinking how good it was to smell the grassy air mixed with the heady perfume of wildflowers. He galloped a wide loop around an immense colony of prairie dogs, and when they thought he was gone, Long Rider pulled his horse to a sliding stop, spun it around on its haunches, and grinned, only to hear the colony's sharp barking sounds and watch them scurry around, realizing they'd been caught off guard.

Gabe continued on, measuring the vastness of the sky and the depth of the nutritious buffalo grass. The grass was so tall it came to his stirrups, and when the breeze stiffened, it waved like a young woman's hair moving to the current of a swift river. The extraordinary height of the grass reminded Gabe that the buffalo had all but been hunted out of southern Wyoming, thanks to the damn transcontinental railroad and the massive westward migration of white people. Along with the passing of the buffalo had gone the nomadic Plains Indians, men whom Gabe considered the finest horsemen and hunters who had ever lived. Gabe could remember when he had gone on buffalo hunts at this time of year as a boy, and how the thrill of hunting buffalo with a bow and arrow could never be equaled or even imagined by anyone who had never had that heart-pounding experience.

But the buffalo were gone from this country now, and soon their range would be covered with longhorn cattle. The Texans were already pushing big herds north into the lush grasslands of Wyoming, Colorado, and the Dakotas. In ten, maybe twenty years, Gabe figured that this country would be nothing but a bunch of huge cattle ranches with longhorn steers covering the same grassy hills that had once been blessed by the native buffalo and the Indian who lived for the hunt.

The image of immense cattle herds did not bring Gabe pleasure, but he was not a man who brooded over things that he could not control. The free-roaming days of the Plains Indian were finished. All the great Sioux chiefs were either reduced to living in bitterness and charity on the white man's reservations, or had been shot or hanged. Now, instead of buffalo hunts, the white soldiers allowed the reservation Indians to stampede domestic cattle into huge pole corrals, where the Indians could shoot them to pieces like fish in a shrinking pond. Long Rider had actually seen the young braves firing crazily into the corrals, and the bawling cattle, riddled and gutshot, collapsing in fear and death. It had made him realize how pitiful things had become for his adopted Indian people.

Right then, Gabe decided that he would spend the summer in Montana and hunt a few buffalo. He would use the skills that his stepfather, Little Wound, had taught him as a boy, and he would make a strong bow and straight arrows. He would fashion arrowheads, too, though he supposed that if he watched the ground over the next few hundred miles on his northern trek he would find many lost arrowheads.

The idea of returning to the life-style of his youth pleased Long Rider so much that he actually smiled, something that was rare. He continued north, content to let each day pass uneventfully and unfold into the next, as it always had unfolded since the beginning of time.

But late the following afternoon, he was disturbed to see a plume of smoke rising to the northwest. By nature he was a curious man and even though he at first resisted the temptation to discover the cause of the smoke, he soon found himself reining his sorrel gelding in that direction. He knew he might come upon a United States Cavalry patrol preparing their evening meal, or even one of the few buffalo hunters or beaver trappers that still roamed this country, men who could not or would not let go of a way of life that had already passed. And finally, there was the possibility that he might also come upon an Indian hunting party. If they were Sioux or any other tribe friendly to those people, Gabe knew that he would be welcomed. But if they were the Crow, then his life might be threatened because the Crow and the Sioux had been enemies before any chief or wiseman could remember.

The possibility of coming upon enemies did not greatly concern Long Rider. He knew his own capabilities and those of his horse, who had already proven itself to possess exceptional speed and stamina. So he could fight or he could run, but either way he was sure that he would survive.

It was nearly sundown when he topped a hill and had a clear view of the place where the fire was burning, and what he saw surprised him for it was a camp of many white men. Men with wagons and horses, tents, and all the equipment that went along with an organized work crew.

Gabe frowned to see that the men had already cut down acres of forest, which was rare in this part of the country. The workingmen had sawed them into identical lengths and stacked them in barn-sized humps. There were dozens of wagons and draft horses, and it suddenly occurred to him that he had stumbled across a crew that was cutting railroad ties.

But for what purpose? The Union Pacific was a couple of days' ride to the south.

Gabe reined his horse away, rode about a mile, and then stopped. If he went on, he would wonder all summer what possible business a crew of men would have cutting railroad ties this far to the north. With a shrug of his broad shoulders, Gabe changed his course and rode on to learn some answers.

"Evenin'!" a big foreman in a leather coat said in greeting. "Step down and share a meal with us, stranger."

Gabe dismounted. There were perhaps fifteen men, and from the looks of the forest they'd cut, they'd been working here at least a month. The man who had just invited him to step down watched Long Rider with considerable interest. He had penetrating blue eyes and a square-jawed face that showed plenty of scars. His nose was fist-busted, and when they shook hands, his palm was as hard and rough as a slab of rock.

"Name is Hank Turner," he said. "I'm foreman of this outfit and you look like a man that could stand a square meal."

"I am hungry," Gabe admitted, studying the foreman before he stepped back and regarded the crew. "And I will have a little food, if you don't mind. A man can get tired of living off buffalo berries, and the game in these parts seems to have been chased out."

"Chased out, hell!" Turner exclaimed. "We've *hunted* them out. Bill Parsons over there is a crack shot and so is Dub Rooney, but he went back to Rawlins on account of he got sick and was shittin' himself to death."

Gabe digested this piece of news without comment or interest.

"Here," Turner said, turning toward the campfire. "Just grab a plate and fill it up. We got nothing but salt pork and plenty of beans and potatoes. Say, you look like a buffalo hunter to me. How'd you like to ride north fifty or sixty miles and slaughter us a couple of buffalo? You could take a wagon and I'd see that Mr. Lydick's railroad pays you good wages."

"I have other things to do," Gabe said without bothering to elaborate. "What railroad are you talking about?"

Turner looked surprised that Gabe did not know about the railroad. "Why, it's Lydick's Railroad that's going north to the buffalo herds, of course! That's what we're doing out here—cuttin' railroad ties. Hell, the advance crew has already pushed as far north as Horse Creek. Know where that is?''

"I do," Gabe said. "What do you mean, 'goin' north to the buffalo herds'?''

"Where on earth have you been? I guess you can't read, huh? You know, you look sorta Indian. You lived with the redskin or somethin'?''

Gabe hid his irritation. "I was raised by the Oglala," he said. "They killed my father before I was even born, and took my mother to become one of their people.''

"Son of a bitch!" Turner said. "I'm surprised your ma didn't just kill herself. She should have, rather than be taken and bred by Indians.''

Gabe turned his back on the man. "I've got no time for the likes of you or any railroad," he announced with disgust as he climbed back into the saddle.

"Well, the hell with you, then!" Turner swore. "Just keep on riding and I hope the Crow come across your uppity ass! They'll fill you so full of arrows you'll look like a damned porkie-pine!''

Gabe touched spurs and galloped away in a hurry. He was sorry he had stopped at the camp, and now he found his curiosity had not been satisfied at all. What had the foreman meant when he'd said they were building a railroad north to the buffalo herds? Why would anyone do that?

Gabe dismissed the entire exchange as an unpleasant bit of conversation that he should have avoided. But still, the man had no reason to lie and if a train was as far north as Horse Creek, it deserved watching.

Without consciously thinking about it, Gabe reined west. Curiosity was a terrible thing when it remained unsatisfied. It was like an itch in the softest place under your foot that had to be scratched, even if that meant going to some inconvenience. Gabe reckoned he was going to find this railroad and learn for himself what it was all about. It seemed mighty strange that anyone would be foolish enough to lay tracks up toward Montana. There weren't any towns or anything. Just more land and some Indian reservations. Damn hard winters and more long grass and the last free grazing buffalo herds in America.

Gabe was a white man, but he thought mostly like the Indians. He carried his mother's Bible in his saddlebags and his happiest memories were of years past when she had taught him to read and write from just that one great book. A little Bible whose every margin was filled with her thoughts, her fears, and her courage.

Hank Turner had just assumed that anyone raised by Sioux was ignorant of reading and writing. Well, making false assumptions and then being stupid enough to state them outright was a good way for anyone to get himself in serious trouble.

Trouble. It seemed to dog Long Rider like fleas after a fat dog. But he guessed that hard times and troubles were more a part of living than good times and fun. Anyone could handle the latter, but the measure of a man's life was how he handled trouble.

Gabe took a deep breath and let his sorrel run into the sunset. Curiosity was indeed an itch that a man needed scratching.

CHAPTER TWO

When Long Rider approached Horse Creek the next morning, he was appalled to see a locomotive and seven railroad cars squatting on a track as if watching the busy crew of workers who were slamming down the iron rails they would soon ride northward. Gabe shook his head and debated whether or not he should approach the construction site. There really wasn't a damn thing that he could do, but still he had to at least speak his piece on the subject of a railroad going north to nowhere. Didn't these people know that there was nothing of interest to the white man up ahead?

Gabe dismounted and watched the crew lay tracks for nearly an hour before he climbed back in the saddle and rode over to Horse Creek to investigate what all the activity was about. Yesterday the man named Hank Turner had said the railroad was heading for the last of the northern buffalo herds. That just didn't tally up in Gabe's mind. But then, none of this did, which was why he was going to have a little talk with the man in charge.

Gabe stopped at the rear car and waited until a short, bandy-legged fella who appeared to be a cook walked over and said, "What do you need, stranger? We're givin' no handouts around here."

"I'm not looking for a handout," Gabe said, his slate gray eyes studying the tracks that led back south. "I'm looking for the ramrod of this outfit."

"He's that loudmouthed son of a bitch over there in the red checkered shirt," the cook said. "But, mister, if I were you, I'd head back to Rawlins and look somewhere else for a job. Working out here under Charlie Bassett isn't my idea of a good time. Every man on this crew is wantin' to quit, but there's no way back to town except walking."

"Why don't they walk?" Gabe asked.

"Hell, man! There's still a few marauding injuns out in this part of the country, not to mention the fact that Bassett has made it clear that no one quits his crew. And those that try will be horsewhipped and let go without their wages."

Gabe shook his head. "Bassett sounds like a hard character to me."

"He is! That's why you'd be best off in riding the hell back to town and looking someplace else for a job."

Gabe reined his horse away. "Much obliged for the warning, but the truth of the matter is that I'm not interested in working for anybody. I'm just wanting to get a little understanding as to why some fool would lay tracks north."

The cook followed him a little ways out from the train. "You'd best not ever let Bassett or any of Lydick's gunnies hear you call him a fool. Aaron Lydick is a very sensitive man."

Gabe said nothing. He had never heard of this Lydick fellow and as he trotted his horse over toward the ramrod he had a feeling that he would be best off to keep things that way. One thing for sure, there was no moss growing under this crew's fannies. They were working off a flat boxcar, three men pulling each of the rails off the car and rushing forward to slam them down on green railroad ties that would warp because they had not been seasoned.

"Move it! Move it! Move it!" Bassett roared at the sweating, grunting crew. "You lazy bastards only laid three miles yesterday, and, by God, Mr. Lydick wants us to average five! So get the iron out of your asses and move it!"

Long Rider pulled his Stetson a little lower over his gray eyes. He could see that this was no time to ask Bassett a few questions, because the man was driving his crew at an outrageous pace.

A wagonload carrying freshly cut railroad ties came storming up from the rear of the line and it damn near ran Gabe and his horse over before he could get out of its way. Two men atop the wagon began to heave the big timbers off the wagon as the vehicle kept moving out in front. Almost as soon as the ties hit the ground, they were snatched up and set in place, only moments before more rails were slammed down and spiked in.

Gabe sat back and watched this precision of labor for nearly an hour. He was impressed with the progress being made, but also his Indian upbringing made it hard for him to understand why the white men were always in such a big hurry. To Gabe's way of thinking, if a job did not get done this day, it would get done tomorrow. The purpose in life was not to slave and worry about the future, but to enjoy each day as much as one could because you never knew if it would be your last.

And how badly these workmen were treated! No Indian would speak to his fellow tribesman in such a way. And if they tried, blood would be shed. Gabe thought the difference between the white men and the red might be that the white men were too ambitious and concerned

with money. For money, they'd do almost anything and
take much abuse. Right now, Charlie Bassett was cursing
and berating his crew in a way that would make a dog
cringe. These men, however, did not seem to pay him
a great deal of attention for they were already grunting,
sweating, and staggering with fatigue.

Suddenly, the bandy-legged cook signaled the noon-
time meal by striking an anvil. At the sound, the crew
stopped working like so many parts of a broken clock
and rushed toward the dining car, where tables and
benches had been nailed to the floor.

Bassett watched them leave on the run, then, for the
first time, he noticed Long Rider sitting on his horse in
the bright morning sunlight and watching him closely.
Bassett said, "If them lazy bastards moved as fast laying
track as they do toward the grub, we'd be halfway to the
Canadian border by now."

Bassett was a tall, rangy man in his early forties. His
face was weather worn and his nose and mouth were thin
and chiseled as if out of sandstone. He had dark eyes
and a wine stain on one cheek which was too large and
high up on his face for his thick black beard to cover.
"You look quick and strong. You seeking honest work?"

"No, sir," Gabe said. "I just wanted to know what
you folks are building a railroad up this way for? Nothing
up there but more empty land and sky."

"Who the hell are you to bother me with your questions?"

"My name is Gabe Conrad."

Bassett stepped up close to his horse. "Well, Gabe,
what we are doing here is really none of your goddamn
business. Now, if you don't want work, then get the hell
out of this camp before I have you run off."

Gabe felt his cheeks burn. "I guess I'll push on, then,"
he said. "But it's fool's work that you're doing and no
good will come of it. I was told by a man named Hank
Turner that you intend to reach the last of the northern

buffalo herds. That would be a mistake. Railroads have already brought about their passing.''

Bassett actually grinned. "Why, if you aren't the great moralizer! What the hell kind of a man are you, anyway! You ride in here and start telling me what I should or should not do. Mister, you got a lot of nerve, I'll say that. And since you are so damn know-it-all, I'll tell you this: Mr. Lydick will make a fortune off this line.''

"How is that possible?''

"All right,'' Bassett said, raising one thick finger. "First off, he's going to take us to the buffalo herds, and then he's going to advertise in the eastern newspapers for hunters. He'll get a thousand dollars a buffalo kill from rich easterners who want to shoot the last of a dying-out breed. He plans to let them use the head for mounting as trophies, but he's going to keep the hide and the meat.''

Gabe blinked. "Why?''

"So he can pack it in ice cars and roll it east and sell it in the best steak houses in Boston, Detroit, and Chicago! He'll get five times the price per pound for buffalo meat as anyone would for beef.''

"In the summer, it would rot before he could get it across the Missouri River,'' Gabe said. "He can't get enough ice.''

"In the summertime, he'll sell all the buffalo meat to the United States Army. They won't pay as high a price, but he'll still get plenty. Mr. Lydick has signed contracts for all he wants to deliver. And we haven't even talked about the robes, but as even you might know, the northernmost herds have the finest robes on this continent. He'll sell those fancy robes in eastern cities for three hundred dollars each.''

Bassett crowed, "Are you beginning to get the picture, Mister Know-It-All? Because if you don't, I'll tell you about how he also plans to buy up land and sell it as small farms. A railroad will always attract suckers looking for cheap farmland.''

"The country north of here isn't any good for farming," Gabe said, feeling angry because he suspected that this Aaron Lydick had everything figured down to the last possible dollar he could wring out of this beautiful northern plains country. ''And you're using such green railroad ties that in a few years this entire track will have to be ripped up.''

"Gee!" Bassett said, mocking him. "What a damn shame! But by then, the farmers will all have been froze or starved out, and we'll have finished off the northern buffalo herds, and you'll be right—there really won't be anything worth riding a train north for.''

Gabe gripped his saddle horn, feeling a tremendous urge to step down and choke that smug, gloating grin off Charlie Bassett's face. "Where can a man find this Aaron Lydick?''

"When he isn't in Washington, D.C., hobnobbin' with United States senators or the top military leaders of this country, you can generally find him in at Summer Creek.''

"Never heard of it.''

"You will," Bassett vowed. "Mr. Lydick has about persuaded the government of this territory to make Summer Creek the seat of central Wyoming's government. It's owned by him, of course. So I guess when this territory finally gains statehood, you might reasonably predict it will become the state capital.''

Gabe shook his head. "It sounds like this Lydick fella has all his ducks lined up in a row and is ready to pull the triggers of both shotgun barrels. He's gonna kill off the buffalo, ruin a bunch of would-be farmers and strip them of their life's savings, then he's going to wind up governor or senator. Is that everything he intends to do? Or does he also have designs on becoming the president of these United States?''

"Say!" Bassett said with a withering smile. "You're not quite as dumb as you look!"

Gabe had heard enough. "Where's Summer Creek?"

"About two days' ride back down this line," Bassett chuckled. "You see, Mr. Lydick, he figures that a town isn't worth spit without a railroad running through the middle of it."

Gabe started to rein his horse away but was stopped as Bassett grabbed his horse's bit. "I think you better step down and work for me, after all. You see, I'm a little short of men and you look strong and fit."

"Let go of my horse," Gabe warned.

Bassett wasn't paying him any attention. "You know, with that Indian-made buffalo vest tied behind your saddle and the way you talk and sort of look away sometimes, you remind me a lot of a damned Sioux brave."

Gabe was not a man to give an order twice. He pulled his gun and pointed it down at the startled man and said, "If you think I'm bluffing, just hang on to that bit one more second and I'll blow your brains across those shiny new rails."

Bassett released the bit and stepped away from the gelding. There was not a trace of fear in his eyes, only anger. "I don't think you'll ever want to cross my path again, Gabe Conrad. If you do, I'll be the one that has a fistful of Colt."

"Thanks for the warning," Gabe said. "And I'll remember that you are a man who talks big but has a secret hankering to die."

Bassett did a double take, then choked, "Now git out of my sight!"

Gabe reined about and rode slowly away.

"Faster!" Bassett shouted.

But Gabe figured he was not going to be run off by anyone. He just kept his horse at a steady walk until he heard the sound of a Winchester being levered, and then the roar of the weapon. Dirt kicked up right beside the sorrel's hind legs and the animal jumped sideways in fear.

Gabe drew his own rifle. The distance was only about fifty yards, but now, when Bassett saw him putting the butt of his weapon to his shoulder, the railroad foreman decided that Gabe meant business, and fired a shot that whistled past Gabe's ear.

In return, Gabe coolly shot the foreman's six-gun and holster from his hip. Bassett cried out in pain and was spun halfway around. The force of Gabe's bullet must have really slammed into him, because he was hobbling when he tried to move. For a moment, he tried to raise his weapon and there was no doubt he would have shot to kill, but when he saw Gabe's own rifle trained on his chest, he had second thoughts and yelled, "There will be another day, Conrad! Another day!"

Gabe jammed his rifle back into his saddle scabbard and touched spurs to his horse's flanks. He figured that Bassett was right about that much. There *would* be another day. This was big country but there were few places to buy supplies, and when they met again, Gabe figured there would be hell to pay. Charlie Bassett was the kind of a man who did not forgive and forget.

When he was out of sight, Long Rider pulled his horse up and let the animal graze a few minutes while he considered what he was going to do next. There was not much point in going to Summer Creek and confronting Aaron Lydick, because it was obvious the man would laugh in his face. So with nothing else to do, Gabe decided to ride north just as he had originally planned. He would spend the summer in the Big Horn Basin country and then, in the fall, he would return and maybe even pay a visit to Bitter Creek.

There was one thing Long Rider was dead certain of, and that was that he would not sit idly by and allow someone to slaughter the last buffalo in America just so he could make a huge profit.

No, sir! The great Sioux and Cheyenne chiefs and their people of the northern plains might be beaten and relegated to a reservation, but Long Rider was legally a white man, and that gave him the right to travel on the open range wherever he wanted, whenever he wanted. And he'd take up the banner against that scheming Aaron Lydick even if he had to do it alone. He'd do it for the buffalo, the poor farmers that were certain to be cheated out of everything they owned, and most of all, for himself so that he could look into a mirror or see his reflection in a clear pool of water and not be ashamed.

Those were still his thoughts two days later when he crossed the Sweetwater River and spotted a large cavalry patrol moving rapidly in his direction. The patrol was led by several officers and civilians, and as they drew nearer, Gabe could see that there were about thirty heavily laden pack horses.

The Captain in charge saw Gabe at once and made a slight correction in his course to bring them together. The senior officer was a handsome fellow with black hair flecked with silver. When he was within twenty feet of Gabe, he raised his gloved hand and shouted, "Companeeee, halt!"

The cavalry drew up and a cloud of dust rolled over them and Gabe, who was studying the group and trying to guess the purpose of their being in this part of the country. Indian trouble? Maybe.

"Who are you?" the captain demanded.

"Gabe Conrad. And who are you?"

"Captain William Stone. We've been up to the Big Horn Basin on patrol."

Gabe looked at the long string of pack animals. "You've also done a little hunting."

"That's correct." The officer studied him with an air of superiority. "A man riding alone up into this country is a man that bears close watching. What is your business up here?''

Gabe took an instant dislike to the man. He'd had his share of run-ins with army officers, and another captain in the United States cavalry named Stanley Price had wrongly sent him into a military stockade for three long years on a trumped-up charge of attempted murder. Captain Stone possessed that same kind of ruthless arrogance, and Long Rider had no intention of being either helpful or respectful. ''Captain,'' he said without a smile, ''I'm just smelling the wildflowers. No law or regulation against a man doing that, is there?''

The officer's tight grin slipped. ''I won't be bandied with,'' he said. ''I want a straight answer.''

''You just got it,'' Gabe told the man. ''I am up here just scouting around. Looking for a little peace and quiet. But it seems I've run into more folks here than I would have most any other place outside the city. Are you aware a damn railroad is being built straight to the north? Can't be more than fifty miles southeast of us.''

''Of course I am!''

The officer glanced sideways at the distinguished-looking man who rode beside him. The man had black hair and was dressed much too expensively to be out on patrol. He was of average height, in his late thirties, and wore soft, expensive leather gloves. His horse was a Thoroughbred, his saddle was ornately tooled, and he wore a fancy gun on his hip. The polished butt of a high-powered hunting rifle protruded from his saddle, and he had a little pouch that contained a European scope the likes of which Gabe had never seen before.

The man stared hard at Gabe and then said, ''That 'damn railroad' you are referring to is *my* railroad, Mr. Conrad. Is there something wrong with it?''

''Everything is wrong with it,'' Gabe said with his customary directness. ''Mr. Bassett told me all about your greedy plans to fleece farmers and destroy the northern buffalo herd. I won't stand for that, and I doubt that the reservation Sioux or Cheyenne will, either. They still rely on buffalo for their existence.''

"Nonsense!" the captain exclaimed. "They are federal government rations. The United States Army, in cooperation with the Indian Agency, also provides them clothing, a school, and medical attention.''

"It does a damn poor job," Gabe said through his teeth. "Anybody that knows anything about the reservation system realizes that it's corrupt. That's why the reservation officials have turned their heads and allowed the Indians to go in small hunting parties to kill buffalo. If Mr. Lydick here wipes the herds out, thousands of Indians may starve or they may go back on the warpath.''

"Are you all finished?" Lydick said with contempt. "Because if you are, then I'll set you straight on a few facts. First, the buffalo are free to roam and free to be hunted by whoever chooses. They don't belong to the Indian any more than this land ever belonged to them.''

"We could argue some about that.''

"Yes," Lydick said, "but where would that get us? You have the look and sound of an Indian lover. And while I'm no Indian hater, I believe the problem is that the Indian is being overly coddled.''

"Coddled! All they want—''

"Is their old way of life," Lydick snapped. "And that is gone. It will never come back. You cannot and will not stop progress or the evolution of civilizations. Stronger peoples have always either massacred their weaker neighbors or else enslaved them. This is no different.''

Gabe said, "Do you know the meaning of a treaty? It is a sworn and written document that two sides use to settle their differences. The Indian kept his side of the deal—always. But the white men made their treaties and then broke them, every one.''

"Circumstances change things constantly. If the treaties were made with good intentions but—''

"But hell!" Gabe said. "I hope you know that your
railroad is heading straight for reservation lands. There
has been so much corruption that the public is starting
to take the side of the red man. That means that I doubt
even you can drive rails across a reservation."

"I concede to your observation," Lydick said. "And,
in fact, my railroad, at great additional expense, will
circumvent the reservation land on its western border.
That makes it legal. I leave the moral issues up to our
congressional leaders, who are the elected conscience of
this country."

Captain Stone had heard enough. "Mr. Lydick is the
guest of the United States Army and has entered into
legal and binding contracts to supply our troops with
buffalo meat. In exchange, we pay him and also provide
protection against Indian deprivations or any other threat.
Is that understood?"

Gabe nodded. "How much is your personal cut off
this deal, Captain?"

Captain Stone bristled with outrage. "If you were under my command, I'd have you sent to the stockade, and
then you'd be court-martialed for contempt of an officer."

"Well," Gabe said, lifting his reins. "At least you'd
have the charges down right."

Lydick interrupted. "What is your *real* name?"

"Gabe Conrad."

"No," the railroad builder said. "It seems to me that
I've read about you. You are known among the Sioux
and their enemies by another name. In fact, I believe
you are rather famous and a close friend of Crazy Horse."

Captain Stone blinked. "Maybe you had better come
along with us to the fort to answer a few questions."

Gabe shook his head. "I've done nothing wrong and
I'm not being sought by anyone. You have no reason to
take me into custody."

When Captain Stone hesitated, Lydick said, "I believe his name is Long Rider! Have you heard that name before, Captain Stone?"

It was clear from Stone's expression that he had. "Sergeant!" he barked. "Place this man under arrest!"

Gabe could have drawn his Colt and shot the sergeant, Lydick, and the captain before the soldiers reacted and killed him, but that was not going to help any. "I demand to know what the charges are against me!"

Stone smiled maliciously. "I don't know yet, but by the time we reach the fort, I'll think of something."

Gabe's Colt was dragged from its holster and his rifle was also taken. When the sergeant pulled a length of rope from his saddlebag, Gabe shook his head. "I won't be bound."

The sergeant looked into Gabe's eyes and swallowed. "Sir? He can't get away from us if I toss a rope around his horse's neck and string it between a couple of us."

"Very well," Stone said. "We will do it that way. But one false move, Long Rider, and I will have you bound hand and foot and tied across your saddle. Is that understood?"

Gabe did not trust himself to speak so he nodded his head. He saw Captain Stone lift his arm and call for his troopers to move on. He looked at Aaron Lydick's face and he knew the rich railroad man was laughing inside as two ropes were placed over his sorrel's head and soldiers pressed in close so that there was no chance for him to bolt and run.

"Who is the fort's commanding officer?" Gabe demanded.

Captain Stone actually laughed outright. "As a matter of fact, *I* am acting in command for Major John Pinkerton, who has taken a business trip to Washington, D.C. The major is a close personal friend of Mr. Lydick's and is, in fact, getting the necessary contracts signed to deliver all the buffalo meat he can supply. Any other questions?''

The muscles of Gabe's jaw stretched as tight as lengths of rawhide, and he said nothing more as they rode south. No longer did he smell the perfume of the wildflowers or feel the warmth of the sun upon his back and think about how good it was to be free and alive.

No more would he think about leaving everything behind and spending an idyllic summer in the Big Horn Basin country. Now his thoughts were focused on some way to thwart the ruthless plans of the army and Aaron Lydick.

CHAPTER THREE

Fort York rested just west of the Medicine Bow River and was a typical stockade with pine-log walls placed on end reaching a height of about ten feet. As Gabe approached it from the northwest, he could see that it was small and very unlikely to garrison and protect more than a hundred soldiers and civilians. Fields of new row crops surrounded the outside walls, and Gabe saw women and children hauling water up from the river and then carefully tending the neat rows of premature corn stalks, tomatoes, and whatever else they had planted. The gardens were all protected from rabbits and other varmints by mesh netting, and someone had even tied colorful cloth ribbons on the mesh fences to keep away the crows and other marauding birds.

Even though the fort was small, Gabe had to admit that whoever had laid it out knew what he was doing from a military point of view. Fort York rested on the very crown of a knoll just a quarter-mile west of the pretty Medicine Bow River. From every side that Gabe could see, there was a long uphill slope to the fort that would offer the defenders a clear field of fire. With the river close by, Gabe was sure that there was at least one shallow water well inside the fort and that, during the wintertime, the cottonwood forests along the riverfront would give the inhabitants plenty of accessible wood to burn.

Ten or fifteen miles to the east, the snow-capped Laramie Mountains lifted majestically toward an azure sky, and to the west, the land was high and semi-desert, with rolling hills covered with both grass and sage. Miles to the south, the Rocky Mountains stood in hazy review and Gabe was sure that those mountains helped form a warm cup that would protect this valley setting from the worst of the blizzards and winter winds.

"I'm going to have to do something about those damn cloth streamers," Captain Stone complained. "Every time I return from patrol, the fort looks like a carnival instead of a military outpost."

Lydick shrugged. "What can you do about them? If the women and children don't put them up, the birds will eat their seedlings. And you know how much Major Pinkerton's wife sets store by fresh corn and tomatoes. As a matter of fact, I am rather partial to them myself. If I were you, my friend, that is one nest of eggs I would not disturb."

The captain scowled. "Sometimes I think that it is Mrs. Pinkerton who commands this fort and makes all the decisions while her husband is away."

Lydick cast a meaningful glance at Gabe, and the captain lapsed into a glowering silence as the gate guards scurried about to draw open the big fortress gates while they were still nearly a mile away.

"There's Mrs. Holly Brown," Lydick said. "I think I'll ride over and extend my greetings."

Gabe saw a tall, graceful woman in her early twenties

with a hoe in her fists. The woman was smiling and talking to several women and children around her. She was fair skinned and very lovely, with long brown hair tied up in a bun behind her head. When she dropped the hoe and joined the others who came to greet the returning patrol, Gabe admired the way she seemed to float across the ground. She moved like a sleek cat, although she was not especially slender.

Long Rider watched as Aaron Lydick pulled his fine-looking horse to a standstill and then dismounted with surprising grace considering his bulk to speak to the young woman. She smiled, but though they were at a considerable distance, Gabe thought the smile lacked real warmth in spite of the flourish that Lydick was giving their reunion.

"How long will I be detained here?" Gabe asked.

"As long as it takes to make sure you aren't in some kind of trouble with the authorities and were trying to vanish to the north."

"I'm not wanted by anyone," Gabe said. "And I won't be locked in your stockade."

"Whatever I decide will be done with you *will* be done," Stone said, giving Long Rider a hard look. "As far as the stockade goes, if you give me your word of honor you'll not try to escape this fort, then I'll grant you freedom of movement. Otherwise . . ."

Gabe inwardly boiled at the thought that he would have to give his word about consenting to an injustice and yet . . . yet he had no choice but to accept the captain's offer. "I'll give you two weeks," he said.

Stone chuckled and it was not a nice sound. "Long Rider, it might be two *months* before I am convinced that you're not a fugitive of the law. But we'll just take things one day at a time. I will tell you this. Your horse will be kept with the rest of our stock, though he will not be ridden. Your saddle, rifle, bridle, and gear will be kept under lock and key as will your weapons."

"I thought the law of this land gave a man the right to keep and bear arms."

"Not on a military outpost," Captain Stone said. "Besides, you'll be protected from all harm here. Why would you need weapons?"

Gabe lapsed into silence. Stone was baiting him. Trying to get him to strike out in anger so he could be put in the stockade. Well, Gabe had no intention of playing into the man's hands so he just rode along tight-lipped, wondering what he was going to do with himself at Fort York for a couple of weeks or months. He was beginning to regret the decision to ever get himself involved in this mess. But on the other hand, if he intended to stop Lydick's railroad and plans to harvest the buffalo herds to the north, he could not be in a better position to gain an insider's knowledge.

"Let me give you a piece of good advice," the captain said, breaking his thoughts in a low voice that was not meant to be heard by anyone except Long Rider. "Despite your poor start with both myself and Mr. Lydick, you can either get smart and maybe even profit here, or you can wind up behind bars. It's your choice."

Gabe would have liked to ask the officer in what way he could possibly "profit" at Fort York, but before he could phrase the question, two children about eight and twelve years old came running up to wave and shout at their father. Gabe saw their mother and the woman who was obviously Captain Stone's wife also wave in greeting. She was short and a little on the plump side, but still pretty, with curly brown hair and a nice smile.

"You have a nice-looking family, Captain," Gabe said as they rode into the fort and dismounted.

"That I do," the captain agreed, taking his children up in his arms and giving each a hug before he kissed his wife on the cheek and said, "Mrs. Stone, this is Long Rider. He is an Indian lover and, therefore, a man not to be completely trusted. But I have trusted him enough to give him the freedom to move about so long as he behaves himself, is respectful of the women, and obeys my orders.''

Mrs. Stone gave Long Rider a curious glance. ''You come under strange circumstances, sir. I hope that you will soon leave unfettered by those same circumstances.''

''I will, ma'am,'' Gabe said. ''I am delighted to make your acquaintance and that of your children.''

Mrs. Stone nodded, then, taking her husband's arm while he handed his reins to a private, she led the captain away, calling, ''Come along, children!''

The older son went obediently enough but the younger one paused and stared at Gabe as if he were a curiosity. ''Are you an injun?'' he asked finally.

''No,'' Gabe said, loosening his horse's cinch.

''You sort of look like one. You're dark like them and you wear buckskins. That vest even has an Indian picture on it.''

''I was raised by the Oglala,'' Gabe said, squatting down on his heels so that he could look the boy in the eye. ''I could tell you many things about the Indians, but I'm afraid your father would not approve.''

''No, he wouldn't like it at all.''

''That's too bad,'' Gabe said. ''But maybe I'll tell you a few Indian stories sometime. Would you like that?''

The boy nodded. ''Do you have a tomahawk?''

''No.''

''Any scalps?''

Gabe shook his head.

The boy slumped with disappointment and just before he ran after his family, he said with disgust, ''Then I don't think there's a derned thing you could tell or show me!''

Gabe allowed himself a smile, then stood up to see Aaron Lydick and Mrs. Brown walk past him. Lydick was still talking when they stopped at the commander's office. Holly Brown glanced in Long Rider's direction and their eyes locked for a second before the woman returned her attention to the railroad builder.

"Conrad? Follow me," a sergeant ordered. "I'll show you where to put your horse, and then I'm supposed to lock up your gear. You'll be sleeping in the sick bay, which also serves as storeroom."

Gabe nodded and led his horse after the sergeant. The small compound they crossed to the stables was rock hard and spotless. It was ringed by barracks, a blacksmith shop, and officers' housing. There were also a dining hall and several other nondescript buildings, all made of weathered wood. Gabe saw the water well that he had predicted, and up on the inside of the walls of the fort stood four bored-looking sentries on high wooden parapets.

"This fort ever been attacked?" he asked.

"Used to be attacked regularly," the sergeant said. "Hell, all along the Bozeman Trail the forts were under attack. You heard about the Fetterman massacre, didn't you?"

Gabe's eyes hardened. "I have."

"Well, we're farther south so we didn't get hit as bad, but there was trouble aplenty for a while. Now, though, we're just making sure that the Indians stay where they belong. That and playing nursemaid to that railroad Mr. Lydick is building north."

"Why is the Army, at the public's expense, protecting a rich man's greedy scheme to earn even more wealth?"

"Hell if I know," the sergeant said. "When you're an enlisted man in the United States Army, you learn to say 'yes sir!' and never ask questions."

Gabe understood that plenty well enough. The sergeant was a career man all the way and he wasn't about to jeopardize his retirement by raising any tough issues. If Gabe wanted information, he was going to have to find someone other than a soldier to provide it.

• • •

Holly Brown finished the day's washing and carried the heavy tub of wet officer's clothes out to her clotheslines. She was perspiring and had a bandanna tied around her head. Wet tendrils of hair stuck to her forehead as her arms corded with muscle began to hang the heavy woolen blues on the sagging clothesline. Since the men and officers had just returned from a long patrol the day before, Holly had all the work she could handle, and even had a waiting list from the enlisted men for their soiled uniforms. Major Pinkerton had made it very clear that, as in all other things on a military post, the officers always came first.

The day was warm but there was a gentle breeze, and Holly knew that, if she managed to get the clothes up before noon, despite their heaviness, they would be dry enough to press this evening. She would work until long past midnight, but her earnings would be considerable over the next few days. It was a good thing, too. Her cupboards were bare and she owed credit at the sutler's store. Everyone knew she was good for the money, but sometimes it was slow in coming. And if she had been an ugly woman, Holly knew she'd have starved for business.

She worked quickly, poking clothespins between her lips and moving down the clothesline with few wasted motions. So intent was she in her work that she did not even see Aaron Lydick until she reached the end of the line and found him studying her with a hungry smile. His unguarded look was so rapacious that she felt her heart quicken and her cheeks burn with embarrassment.

"Ah, Mrs. Brown," Lydick sighed. "You are much too beautiful to be a washerwoman."

"There is nothing beautiful about washing other men's clothes for a living," she said. "But it pays the bills and I take a certain pride in seeing a soldier or officer's tunic properly washed and pressed."

"It's a small and not very important thing, that," Lydick said. "Especially considering how many other talents I suspect you have to offer."

Holly said nothing. She could very well imagine what other "talents" he was thinking about.

Aaron Lydick picked up a pair of wet trousers with obvious distaste, handed them to her, and said, "Please, why can't you accept my help?"

"Because I won't take charity and I will never become dependent upon anyone again," she told him with a tolerant smile. "Really, Mr. Lydick. We've gone through all this before. In fact, a number of times."

"I know. I know and I apologize," he said, holding up his hands, palms outward in an exaggerated gesture of self-defense. "But I could do so much for you."

"I can do for myself," Holly said, furiously pinning up the clothes.

Lydick next reached down and pulled a heavy blue tunic with a lieutenant's bar attached to it. "It's just such a waste of beauty watching you do this drudgery that it pains me greatly. I could help you establish your own business in Summer Creek. I'm offering you the chance to own a thriving business!"

"No, thank you. This is my own thriving business," she said with exasperation as he wiped perspiration from her brow.

"Be serious," he told her. "And if the idea of being in someone's debt is so disagreeable, then allow me to simply advance you a low-interest loan. Pay me back with your profits whenever you can, Mrs. Brown. Now, what would be the harm in that arrangement?"

Holly picked up her washtub and carried it to the next line, her hands working quickly and quite independently of her mind. "Mr. Lydick, I am happy with my station in life for the moment."

He came around in front of her and his eyebrows lifted with disbelief. Waving at the dripping clothesline, he said, "How can you possibly be happy since your husband died on patrol last fall and you were forced to wash clothes for a living? You have no security. No future here at Fort York. For a woman like you, this is nothing at all."

"It's just fine for me," she replied, giving him her best imitation of a smile. "I'm not the one that's complaining, and neither are the single officers and enlisted men who appreciate my effort."

"Of course they do! They all lust for—"

Holly's eyes flashed and Lydick's outburst died on his lips. "I'm sorry, Mrs. Brown. I did not mean to be rude or insulting but we both know that you are the toast of this fort and that your business is the direct result of men who are captivated by your charm and beauty."

"I do my job well!" Holly snapped. "If I did a poor job on their dress uniforms and they failed daily inspection, my looks or disposition wouldn't stand for anything. They'd find someone else to do their laundry."

Lydick removed his cream-colored Stetson and ran his fingers through his thick, black hair, which he combed straight back and neatly parted in the center. He had dark eyes and now they shuttered just slightly. "Mrs. Brown," he began in a regretful tone, "I didn't want to say this but I think you should be warned that there is trouble on your horizon here at Fort York."

Holly had been stooping to get another piece of her laundry to hang but the man's words brought her up short. Clothes forgotten, she straightened and said, "What are you talking about?"

"Could we sit down in the shade someplace?" Lydick asked, mopping his own brow before returning his Stetson to his head.

"I'm sorry, but I have to get these clothes hung right now. Please tell me what kind of trouble you are referring to as being on my horizon."

"It has to do with your civilian status and the fact that

this is an Army post with Army housing for married officers.''

Holly felt a hard place knot in her stomach. "I am the widow of an officer of the United States Army," she said. "I am not a civilian."

"Oh, but you are!" Lydick said gently and with a sad smile. "You see, it certainly is not my decision and I think it's entirely unfair, Mrs. Brown. I mean, your husband did give his life for his country. But still, it's obvious that this post is far too small for the number of families here, and Captain Stone is painfully aware there are families who need your residence."

Holly turned away. She *knew* who had put this bee in Captain Stone's empty bonnet. She also knew that Aaron had just played his hole card and the game had gotten dirty. "So," she said in a voice that trembled with anger, "I don't suppose you'd know about how long I have left here before I am evicted?"

"Evicted? Well, that is a rather harsh term for relocation. Besides, I don't think there is anything immediate."

Holly's hands dropped to her sides. She had always known that Lydick would manage to put her back to the wall because he got whatever he wanted in life—and he wanted her very badly.

"Mrs. Brown? Are you all right?"

"Yes," she said, her mind trying to grapple with the prospect of having nowhere to go and not much ready cash to get there, thanks to her late husband's considerable gambling debts, many of which she still had not been able to pay. For the record, the Army inquiry had determined that Lieutenant Peter Brown had drowned in an attempt to find a good river crossing, but Holly had heard rumors that her husband had been pulled from his tent, gagged, and tied hand and foot before being drowned because he refused to pay off his gambling debts. It was not a rumor that she wished to believe, but given her husband's reckless disregard for responsibility, it was believable.

Holly suddenly felt crushed and defeated while the man before her seemed invincible and even, God help her, an attractive salvation from the loneliness and poverty that was her lot at Fort York. All her life she had wished for a little money and for some kind of security. Just a single taste of the finer things that had never been hers to enjoy. Aaron Lydick was rich and she could probably even get him to marry her if she handled him properly. She could finally have that money and peace of mind.

It was not like she would have to live with the man forever. Aaron would tire of her in a few years. As sure as the years passed and her youth and beauty would fade, Aaron would one day discover someone younger and prettier, and then she would be released, probably before she was thirty. There would be a generous and very public divorce settlement because an aspiring politician like him would have to keep up the appearance of being a decent man. Probably, she would be forced to admit adultery or some such outrageous thing before the divorce so that the public's entire sympathy would be for Mr. Aaron Lydick. Public sympathy could get a man elected to office. She knew that and so did Aaron.

"Mrs. Brown," Lydick was saying, "I am sorry if I have upset you. It's just that I thought you needed to be warned of a possible conflict that could necessitate a move. And since you *will* have to move soon, why not to Summer Creek, where I can see that you are protected and where you can establish a flourishing business? We can be friends and I'm sure you would be delighted with the accomodations that you will find."

Holly was dead certain that the only "accommodations" she'd find would be in Aaron Lydick's bed. "Let me think on it," she said, not wishing to pursue the subject right now while her spirits were so low and her defenses down to her ankles.

Her answer pleased him. "Splendid! I'm leaving today, but I'll be back soon. Very soon. I hope that I can assist you in moving to Summer Creek at that time."

"Mr. Lydick?" she blurted.

He had been turning to leave, but now he stopped. "Yes, my dear woman?"

"What could I do in Summer Creek?" she asked impulsively. "Really."

The question seemed to catch him by surprise. "Well . . . let's see," he said, hedging his answer as his mind raced. "I'd not advise doing laundry. We do have a Chinaman and his family, who are excellent. . . . However, I'm sure that they could be persuaded to sell their business very, very reasonably if—"

"No!" Holly surprised even herself with the vehemence behind her answer. But she knew that Aaron would not have any hestitation whatsoever in running a poor Chinese family out of Summer Creek if there was no other way to get her tangled into his web.

"All right, then," Aaron said, "you might consider opening a millinery shop. There are quite a few ladies in town. If you also ran a full line of cloth and sewing things I believe you could do very nicely. And I understand you are an expert seamstress, so that would also work right in with such a business."

Lydick seemed exceedingly pleased with himself. "Yes! You would be very successful at such an enterprise."

Holly tried not to reveal the sudden flicker of excitement she felt rise up inside of her. In truth, while she had many friends here at Fort York, she longed to live in a frontier town with a church and even a school where children played and sang at recess. A town where there were stores to shop in and civic clubs and groups where people worked together to better their lives and their own community.

"Tell me about Summer Creek," she said, forgetting her wash. "It has such a fine-sounding name. Is it nice? How many women live there? Is there a church and a school?"

Lydick sighed. "I'm afraid there are only about fifty women there now, but more are coming every week. You see, I've built a railroad line up from the Union Pacific. Summer Creek is growing very fast. We need someone like you to set an example. To motivate the other women and make our town a real community. Quite honestly, Mrs. Brown, I am going to do everything within my power to see that Summer Creek becomes the territorial and, eventually, the state capital. To do that, we need respectable but also energetic and high-minded ladies like yourself."

Lydick touched her shoulder. "Mrs. Brown," he said, "I know that you are very, very proud. That is one of the things that I most admire about you. But pride cometh before a fall and stubborn pride is not a virtue but a sin. Please understand that, if you allow me to help you in Summer Creek, you in turn will be helping me see that fine young community that I call home become a thriving metropolis. A place where anyone would want to live and raise their children. Help us, Mrs. Brown."

Holly looked into his eyes and she knew he was lying through his teeth but she found herself nodding her head. "All right," she decided. "Since I'm sure that I will be evicted now that the issue of housing is on Captain Stone's mind, then I might as well come to Summer Creek. I have no living family. I have no particular place to go."

Aaron smiled for his victory had been won. He touched her cheek and a tendril of her hair. "A wise decision, Holly. One you'll never regret. I'll have a man bring a wagon over from Summer Creek to transport your belongings. I'll personally take you away in my carriage."

"For appearance' sake," she told him, "I'd rather stay with my things. I just would feel better if you met me there instead of coming to Fort York."

He leaned forward and kissed her cheek. "Of course. Good-bye."

She watched him walk away and he was a fine figure of a man. He walked straight and proud and very confidently. Any woman would consider him a prize. But Holly felt no joy inside, only emptiness. He had set his sights on her and she had been just as determined that she would not become his plaything. But now, he had won because he had taken away all her alternatives.

Holly brushed a tear from her eye and snatched up more clothes to hang. She worked so hard that sweat stung her eyes but she didn't care. Well, Holly thought, at least I have sold myself to a very high bidder.

CHAPTER FOUR

The day after he arrived at Fort York, Long Rider was brushing his sorrel gelding when he saw three big soldiers enter the barn. At first, he paid them no attention but when they approached him walking shoulder to shoulder, he knew that their arrival spelled trouble. Gabe kept right on currying his horse as if he were totally absorbed in his work.

"I heard you're called Long Rider," a beefy sergeant who stood in the center drawled, "and that you rode with Red Cloud and Crazy Horse against the Army."

Gabe kept on brushing. "What I have done is my business, Sergeant."

The sergeant's fists balled at his sides and when he stepped forward, the other two men came along with him like a pair of bookends. "All three of us lost friends at the Little Big Horn. We don't like to hear that kind of talk from anyone."

"I lost friends at that battle, too," Gabe said, still not

looking up and hoping to avoid trouble. "Both red men and white."

"But more red men," a corporal said with contempt. "You look like a redskin and you smell like one."

Now Gabe straightened, the wire currycomb still in his hand. "And how do Indians smell?" he asked quietly.

"Like pigs!"

Gabe knew they expected him to react, so he did nothing but shrug his broad shoulders and say, "Oh."

The three soldiers were caught off guard. Finally the sergeant said, "That's all you've got to say?"

"You're entitled to your opinion, as I am to mine."

"And what is your opinion?" the sergeant demanded. "Or are you too scared to tell us?"

Gabe studied the trio. "Look," he said, "I don't like you and you don't like me. So why don't we leave it at that?"

"You're a goddamn Indian-lovin' son of a bitch."

The Indians had taught Long Rider a thing or two about living, and one of the things he had always held to be good advice was to draw a fair line and then to allow nobody to trample across it. The sergeant had just crossed the line when he'd called Gabe's mother a bitch.

Gabe brought the wire currycomb up, drove its sharp bristles into the sergeant's face, and raked flesh from the point of his jaw clear up to his hairline. One moment the sergeant was staring at him, the very next instant his eyes were covered with blood and he was screaming in pain.

Gabe's attack was so swift and disabling that it caught the other two men off guard and staring in amazement. Gabe's hand slammed the currycomb against the slack jaws of one soldier and the man was knocked to the earth floor. The corporal, however, had recovered, and with a low growl, had thrown his powerful arms around Gabe, pinning him in a crushing embrace.

"Git him!" the corporal grunted as his two companions struggled to regain their senses.

Gabe had no intention of allowing himself to be pinioned helplessly. He butted his chin into the corporal's nose, and as it cracked, blood gushed.

The corporal cried out in pain and Gabe managed to tear loose and then drive two powerful hooks to the man's ribs. The sergeant, however, had recovered and kicked Gabe in the side of the knee, sending him to the floor. They rolled. The sorrel gelding was jumping and rearing against its rope as Gabe and the sergeant struggled under its feet. Gabe came out on top and sledged the sergeant in the throat, and the man strangled and began to choke.

The corporal was still moaning and cupping his broken nose and cradling his ribs with the other. Gabe ignored him and turned on the third soldier, who, seeing his friends both completely taken out of the fight, showed the most sense of all by turning on his heels and running out the door.

The fight was over and it had not lasted ten seconds.

"Easy, boy," Gabe said to his horse. "Easy."

The animal calmed to Long Rider's gentle voice and touch although it was clear that it smelled the blood because it trembled.

"Goddamn you!" the corporal moaned. "You broke my nose!"

"Maybe that will keep you from sticking it into other men's business," Gabe said. "If there is a doctor on the post, he can set it straight. Otherwise, I can do it."

"The hell you can!" The corporal staggered to his feet and, bent over with pain, he stumbled out the door.

Gabe looked down at the sergeant who had turned blue in the face but now seemed to be breathing again and regaining normal color. "I didn't want to do that," he explained, "but you boys gave me little choice. Need a drink of water or anything?"

The sergeant looked up at him through hate-filled eyes. "You're . . . you're a dead man!"

"Sorry to hear that," Gabe said, as he began to brush his horse again. "But the next time you come looking for trouble, bring some men."

The next afternoon, Long Rider sat beside the corral with his back against a fence post and observed the people and their activities. A work party of about ten soldiers were building a new barracks and the sound of their hammers echoed across the valley. Two women were chatting in the shade of a building and several children were playing catch with an old hide-bound ball of some sort. An old dog was trotting across the compound trying to look as if it had a reason to be going someplace, and a second work party of soldiers were preparing to go out and gather firewood from among the cottonwood groves down by the Medicine Bow River.

But the most interesting sight and the one that absorbed most of Gabe's attention was that of Mrs. Holly Brown trying to finish her laundry hanging while the rich Aaron Lydick pestered her about something or other. Because of the hammering and the distance that separated them, Gabe could not overhear the conversation, but he figured he could pretty well guess the nature of their discussion. Lydick was badgering the beautiful young woman about something, and for a while she resisted, but then Gabe saw her hands drop to her sides in a gesture that said as clear as words that she had lost the argument. And when Lydick actually kissed her cheek and then turned on his heel with a look of pure triumph, Gabe knew in his heart that the rich man had done something to change Holly Brown's life, and probably for the worse.

Gabe might have walked over and struck up a conversation with the woman except that Lydick had spotted him and was coming in his direction.

"Afternoon, Long Rider," the railroad man said, just as if they were long-standing friends.

"I heard you had a little trouble out in the barn yesterday."

"A little," Gabe admitted.

"I understand that you are going to be a dead man before tomorrow morning. You can't whip the entire garrison."

"I know that," Gabe said, thinking that he had no choice but to try and escape but that he'd be watched by everyone and that escape was next to impossible.

Lydick studied him closely. "Hell, I don't see a mark on your face and the other three look as if they were attacked by a horde of Apache. You're really something, Long Rider. A man that knows how to handle himself. I like that. I could use someone like you on my side, instead of facing me as an opponent."

"We just see things different," Long Rider told him. "There's nothing personal about it."

Lydick chuckled. "I like that! You're right. It's all business—at least for me it is."

When Gabe said nothing, Lydick did not go away but seemed inclined to talk. "You know, earlier this morning, I was trying to remember how you got your name. Didn't you, as a boy, ride some incredibly long distance to bring help for your people?"

"Something like that," Gabe said, not bothering to look up at the man.

Lydick tugged up the creases of his tailored pants, then squatted on his heels so they were at eye level. "You know, you've gotten yourself into sort of a mess here. I think you might get tossed in the stockade before this is over."

Gabe looked at him almost with amusement. "So are you going to lose sleep over that, or what?"

Lydick chuckled. "You're a man with a sense of humor. I like that, too! It's such a shame that far too many men take themselves so damned seriously. But I have the feeling that you are a man that puts things into the proper perspective and knows how to make them work out for the best. Not always the way you'd exactly like, but for the best.''

Lydick winked. "Isn't that true?"

"No," Gabe said, "it isn't. What are you after— besides that pretty widow woman hanging her wash?''

"You don't miss much, do you?" Lydick said. "The truth of it is that I appreciate the talent of everyone I meet. You know, we all have talents. I suspect you have unique talents because you are a white man, yet you've been raised as an Indian. That means that you know the Indian way. Know how they think and reason. Isn't that so?''

"I understand them as well as one man ever 'stands another," Long Rider said. "You are still playing games. What is it that you want from me?''

"Games?" Lydick shook his head. "I don't play games. No sir. What I really do well is make money, and the way to make money is to know how to handle people. All kinds of people. Senators, generals, heads of government committees and departments right on down to the little man. Men like you, Long Rider.''

"You don't know the first thing about handling men like me," Gabe told him. "You and I are from two different worlds.''

"That is true," Lydick said, holding up his finger. "But we both have things we want in this life, and I know what you want because you've already told me. You want to help your adopted Indian people. I want to harvest the buffalo and, in your mind, the two things are at odds.''

"They'd be at odds in anyone's mind," Gabe said. "Get to the point.''

"The point is this. You are unique in that you can help me smooth things over with the Indians. In exchange for that, I will help you—and them.''

"You're not making sense," Gabe said.

"Listen closer, then. If you help me with the Indians—keep them peaceful and also assist me in finding the buffalo I need to fulfill my contracts both back east and with the Army—then I'll save your skin by getting you out of Fort York today and also make you a nice pile of money."

"Not interested."

"You have to be interested in living," Lydick said. "And I'll add something else to sweeten the pot. Help me and I'll donate a percentage of my gross profits to the Indian people. You can choose which tribes. You can even have the credit."

Gabe shook his head. "Why should the Indians settle for a percentage of your slaughter profits when they believe they own all the buffalo?"

Lydick said, "Let me lay it out clear for you. As I've already explained, the buffalo herds belong to anyone who can reach them and kill them. And I'll be very frank, Long Rider. If I don't harvest them for their meat, hides, and their prize heads, then someone else—someone who will not share a penny of the profits with the Indian people—definitely will."

"So," Gabe said, "You're warning me that I can either work with you and get a piece of the cake, or get nothing because it will happen, anyway."

"That's right. You see, I am not the only man in this territory who sees the possibility of a large profit in buffalo hides and meat. I just happen to be the first one to have the money and the energy to execute the idea."

"What about the farm land you're going to promote up north? You know that it is a scheme that can't help but fail."

"I know nothing of the sort!" Lydick exclaimed. "And neither do you. What I'm doing is offering something for sale. I make no promises as to soil or weather or the length of a growing season. I simply offer cheap land and a railroad to a town as yet to be named. Those who have the vision, the knowledge, and the sheer guts to make it work will succeed; the rest will fail. That is up to them, not you or I.''

Gabe looked into the man's eyes for a long moment and then shook his head. ''I've met promoters before but you take the cake.''

''I consider that a compliment. Listen, I am rich and successful and I've just made you an offer that will save your life and help the Indian people. It must be very obvious that I will do this project with or without your cooperation. All the Washington deals are done and the machinery is in motion. I haven't left a stone unturned. The contracts for delivery of meat and hides are signed. You, Long Rider, serve only to make the task easier.''

''What percentage for the Indians?''

''Ten.''

''Thirty.''

Lydick chuckled. ''That's ridiculous. I couldn't make a profit on that.''

Gabe was not a devious man but was a practical one. He knew that he could either refuse and probably get murdered before he could escape Fort York, or he could agree and have an opportunity to get inside Lydick's operation that would not come his way again.

''Twenty percent and I'll be your go-between with the Sioux and the Cheyenne. I can't make any promises about the Crow. They are my people's enemies.''

''Fifteen percent,'' Lydick said. ''It will still amount to tens of thousands of dollars. I will even work to increase the food, clothing, and medical expenditures for the Sioux. I have the influence to do that, you know.''

Gabe did not doubt those words. ''Let's spell out our agreement real plain.''

''Fine. But why don't you come with me to Summer Creek and we can spend some time together and iron out every detail. If it will make you feel better, I will even have my lawyer write up an agreement and terms.''

"*Your* lawyer?"

"Do you have your own, Long Rider?"

"Of course not. But what about the fact that I'm confined to this fort?"

"I'll make the arrangements," the railroad man said. "It will only take a minute and you will have your weapons and your horse back in your possession immediately."

"When you say you have influence, you really mean it."

Lydick's smile faded. "Damn right, I do. I can make men—or break them. You remember that, Long Rider. I want no trouble between us. I've heard the stories and I know you can be a hard enemy. I prefer to work with you rather than against you. It's as simple as that and the fact that you have those unique talents and a background that will prove so useful to my plans. Do we have an understanding?"

Gabe thought about Holly Brown and how he had just seen her give in to this man's persuasive powers just as he was doing. "Yes."

"Excellent! I'll go have a talk with Captain Stone this minute. Prepare to leave within the hour."

Gabe watched the man walk away and then, on a whim, he headed across the compound to speak to Holly Brown. Whether or not she knew it, they now had something in common.

"Good afternoon, ma'am," he said, tipping his hat.

Holly looked across the line of dripping clothes at the tall, deeply tanned young man. He was ruggedly handsome, a fact she'd noticed since the moment she'd first laid eyes on him. He had sand-colored hair and his slate gray eyes possessed both a mesmerizing and very tranquil quality. And yet she had heard how badly he had injured three soldiers yesterday, one of them being Sergeant Beason, one of the toughest men in the Army. Holly hadn't believed it possible until now, when she looked at this man closely.

Holly brushed back the damp hair from her forehead and smiled. "Hello."

"My name is Gabe Conrad," he said. "And I'm told yours is Mrs. Holly Brown."

"That's true," she said, remembering that she had also heard rumors that this man would be dead before tomorrow's sunrise and wanting to warn him of his danger. "I understand you are called Long Rider by the Oglala."

"Just lately, I've been called other names," he confided with a look of youthful amusement. "Names that I would never repeat in a lady's company."

Holly stopped pinning up the clothes. "Are you aware that you have many enemies here?"

"Yes."

"And that they intend to kill you?"

"Yes," he repeated. "That's why I'm leaving Fort York without getting to know you better."

Holly could not hide her surprise at his frankness. "Mr. Conrad, are you always so blunt?"

"Most of the time," he admitted. "I'm going to Summer Creek with Aaron Lydick. Am I correct in guessing that you are, too?"

Holly blinked. "What makes you think I might be?"

"I don't know. It's just that I saw you talking to him and somehow got that impression. I thought that we might get better acquainted there."

Holly almost laughed out loud. "You *are* bold! But let me explain something. I am going at the invitation of Mr. Lydick. And while he certainly has no claim on my attentions, I have a suspicion that he would not approve of your calling on me in his town."

"I don't care about that," Gabe said. "You see, we both have some things in common. We are caught here in a bad spot and need some way out. Aaron Lydick was our only hope, so we're going.''

"You take a great deal for granted, Mr. Conrad. I don't have any interest in making the acquaintance of strangers and certainly not one that has your violent reputation. And as for my business in Summer Creek, well, Mr. Lydick has graciously offered to help me establish a millinery shop. I've never owned my own business, and I'm excited about the prospect.''

"You have a laundry business right here at Fort York," he said. "And you don't seem to owe anyone any favors.''

Holly felt insulted. "How can you imply that I am placing myself in Aaron Lydick's debt when you yourself have just admitted he is your own salvation?''

"I will always be my own man.''

"And I will be my own woman," she said with a hint of irritation. "Now, if you don't mind, I have more work to do.''

Long Rider watched her pick up her empty laundry tub and start back toward her small Army shack. "I'll see you in Summer Creek," he said as she passed.

"Not if you're smart, you won't!''

Long Rider laughed deep within himself. The Army widow was trying to warn him that Aaron Lydick was possessive and dangerous. Well, he'd already guessed as much and he would be careful. But careful or not, Gabe had a feeling that he wanted to become much better acquainted with Holly Brown.

CHAPTER FIVE

When Long Rider rode out of Fort York he could almost feel the anger his departure brought to many of the soldiers. Sergeant Beason, his face a livid scab from chin to forehead, was at the gate, and when Gabe passed, the sergeant growled, "Another time, Long Rider. There'll be another time."

"You better hope not," Gabe said as he passed outside.

"You don't have many friends back there, do you?" Lydick said with a knowing glance as they galloped away.

"Friends don't come easy to me," Gabe said. "I pretty much like to be left alone, and I treat others the same as I like to be treated."

Lydick said nothing as they rode toward Summer Creek, which Gabe knew was only about eighty miles distant. He sat tall in the saddle and it felt mighty good to be free of Fort York. Lydick also seemed happy to be traveling. He rode well and cut a handsome figure astride his tall Thoroughbred, which had a tremendously long stride and seemed to devour the miles effortlessly.

That night they camped on a small stream, and Lydick produced a bottle of wine, two glasses, along with a couple of meat pies that he had cooked for him at Fort York.

Sitting cross-legged across from each other and watching the fire, Lydick raised his wineglass and said, ''Are you sure you don't want to at least try this imported French wine?''

''I'm sure,'' Gabe said, for he had decided long ago that drink made men weak or foolish.

''Then I may be forced to drink it all by myself,'' the railroad builder said. ''Anyway, here is to a successful partnership between us. One that helps everyone and hurts no one.''

Gabe nodded, though he could not imagine how killing off the northern plains buffalo herds could fail to devastate the Indian peoples.

''You know,'' Lydick said when he had finished his meat pie, ''I was born into a pretty wealthy family and there are a few men who say that I had every advantage. But the truth is, I have made many times over what I eventually inherited from my family. I am what I am because of hard work. I have dedicated myself to wealth and fame.''

Lydick sipped his wine and looked at Gabe, seated impassively across the flames. ''Have you ever dedicated yourself to anything, Long Rider?''

''Yes.''

''What?''

''To revenge the death of my wife and my mother.''

''Tell me more.''

Gabe considered the request and then said, ''They were both murdered in a dawn cavalry charge through a friendly Arapaho village on the Tongue River by an officer named Captain Stanley Price. He shot my wife through the brains and ran my mother through with his sword.''

Gabe shook his head in bitter rememberance. ''I had two little children I was trying to save, one under each arm so I could not help my own family. For a long time after that, I lived for nothing but the day I would kill that man.''

''I guess I don't have to ask if you did or not.''

''No,'' Gabe said. ''You don't. It took me years to track him down. He'd resigned in disgrace and I had to go back to the East to find him. But I did.''

''What happened to your trigger finger?''

Gabe looked down at his right index finger that was twisted sharply outward. ''I can thank that same captain for this.''

''Can you still use a six-gun?''

''What do you think?'' Gabe said.

''I would bet that you use your left hand and a cross draw.''

Gabe neither confirmed or denied that supposition. Actually, after thousands of hours of practice, he had learned to draw and fire with either hand. What he preferred and was fastest at, though, was the cross draw with his left hand streaking across his belly and drawing the gun. He was also pretty sudden using a shoulder holster that could be concealed under his coat or buffalo hide vest.

Lydick said, ''I have a few men that consider themselves pretty quick with a gun. I'll warn you right now that you'd do well not to cross them. I'm sure that they would not be your equal in a fistfight, but with a six-gun, well, that is their only stock and trade.''

''Why do you need to hire professional gunfighters?''

''It's insurance, plain and simple. While I do pride myself on making as few enemies as possible, I find that when you are rich and determined to become even richer, it is inevitable that you will make bad enemies."

Gabe finished his own supper and lay back down on his bedroll to look up at the stars. "I'm surprised that you trust yourself to sleep near me."

"Why not? If you killed me—and I might tell you that I am skilled with a gun myself and a light sleeper— if you did that, the United States Army would track you to the ends of the earth and you'd be stood up before a firing squad. Hell, even worse for a man like you— they'd send you to a federal prison for the rest of your natural life."

"You've got everything figured out down to the small-est detail, don't you?"

"Yeah," Lydick said, pouring himself more wine. "I think so. And I think that I'm going to finally bed Holly Brown this month. I've wanted that woman since the day I first laid eyes on her."

"I can understand why," Gabe said.

"I was afraid you'd say that," Lydick told him, his voice hardening. "I saw you talking to her while I was in Captain Stone's office getting permission for your release. I don't want you around her when she comes to Summer Creek. I don't want you around her at all. Is that understood?"

Gabe raised up on one elbow and looked across the fire. His first impulse was to tell this man that he did not really care what he said because no man could tell him to stay away from a woman unless it was the man's wife. But Gabe bit back his words and held his tongue because, for the time being, there was simply too much at stake to lose over a woman. If he were going to see Holly in Summer Creek, it would have to be on the sly.

Nothing wrong with that, Gabe thought as he settled back down on his bedroll. Sometimes, clandestine meet-ings with a beautiful woman were the most fun of all.

• • •

When they intersected with Lydick's railroad tracks, the rich man said, "Summer Creek is just south of here, about a mile north of the intersection of my tracks with those of the Union Pacific."

"A mile north so that you own the land instead of the Union Pacific, right?"

"That's right." Lydick chuckled smugly to himself. "They were, to say the least, a little upset when I drew up my town site just beyond the northern boundaries of their property. They even threatened to start their own town just south of Summer Creek. I was worried about that. I have money and influence, but not enough to buck the entire Union Pacific. Anyway, I paid a visit to Omaha and we worked out a little arrangement satisfactory to all parties concerned."

"I'm sure you did," Gabe said, standing up in his stirrups and looking straight ahead. "What is this up ahead?"

Lydick frowned. "Looks like someone is in trouble with a broken axle."

Gabe had already formed the same opinion. He could see a wagon ahead, with its axle clearly snapped. A young man and woman were arguing, and then the man hauled off and belted the woman, knocking her completely off her feet.

Gabe touched spurs. If there was one thing he did not tolerate, it was grown men hitting women or children. And not only did the man hit the woman, but he kicked her in the side when she was down. Gabe saw her try to rise, but the man swung his foot back to kick her again.

They were well beyond pistol range, so Gabe shouted, "That's enough of that!"

The couple had not seen them approaching, and now the man bolted for his wagon and yanked out a rifle. He took aim and opened fire on the charging horseman.

Gabe was still a good six hundred yards distant, far out of pistol range, so he slid his horse to a halt and

reached for his own rifle. But he needn't have bothered.
A hundred yards behind and to the right of him, Aaron
Lydick had stopped his horse, grabbed his hunting rifle
and scope, and snapped them together with practiced
speed. Before the young hothead could scatter any more
lead at Gabe, Lydick knelt, rested his left elbow on his
left knee, and carefully squeezed off a shot.

Gabe was stunned to see the young man throw his
arms up in the air, sending the rifle flying as a blossom
of crimson opened widely across his chest. The man
seemed to stare upward at the sun. His entire body quiv-
ered, and then he pitched over onto his face and was
dead.

For a long moment, the only sound that could be heard
rolling across the Wyoming grass-covered hills was the
echo of Lydick's high-powered hunting rifle, until Lydick
swore with delight. "Jesus Christ! What a shot!"

Gabe turned to stare at Lydick in disbelief as the railroad man carefully removed the scope from his custom-
made hunting rifle and packed it into its special leather
case.

Meanwhile, the woman had not moved, and it occurred
to Gabe that the kick she'd taken might have driven
busted ribs into her heart or lungs and actually killed her.
He jammed his scarred and well-used Winchester back
into his saddle scabbard and remounted his horse.

Lydick said, "Long Rider, let's decide right here and
now that it was *you* that killed that man and saved the
woman. I can't afford to have my name associated with
a death."

"But I didn't even get off a round."

Lydick slid his own rifle back into its fancy scabbard
before riding up to him. "You and I know that, but the
girl was hurt and lying facedown. She saw you coming
and will assume you killed that man."

"What about the coroner?" Gabe asked, gesturing
toward the polished butt of the man's big hunting rifle.

"That cannon of yours probably blew a hole through his chest big enough to slide my fist through."

Lydick, as Gabe expected, had a ready answer. "Sometimes a man loads his own cartridges and uses more powder than he should. That's what you did with that Winchester of yours. If there are any questions, I'll make sure they aren't asked by the mortician. Is that clear?"

"Yeah," Long Rider said. "I guess it is."

Lydick was not pleased with himself. "I should have let you kill the fool but it was a challenging shot, and I just couldn't resist. The important thing to remember is that you would have killed him if I hadn't."

"I would have," Gabe admitted.

"Why don't you go take care of the young woman?" Lydick suggested. "I'll send out a blacksmith to repair that broken axle. I'd rather not be involved at all with this. Besides that, I'm late for other business. Get that poor woman into Summer Creek and let me know what she is doing out here alone with a brute like that. Probably the best thing you can do for her now is to bury her man and I'll buy her a one-way train ticket down the line in either direction."

"Sounds reasonable," Gabe said. "I'll take care of things."

Lydick studied the girl. "She's not a bad looker, at least from a distance she isn't. You might want me to wait until tomorrow to send out the blacksmith."

"With her husband just shot through the chest?"

"Never take appearances for granted," Lydick said. "They can be very deceptive."

"Then why don't you claim the kill and go make yourself her hero?"

"Like I said," Lydick answered, "I got business to take care of. Besides, I've staked a claim to Holly Brown and I'd like you to find a similar distraction. Maybe we all got lucky just now."

"Not that poor devil who just had his heart blown through his backbone," Gabe said, climbing into the saddle.

But Lydick wasn't listening. "Good luck," he said with a wave of his hand as he rode away.

Gabe loped his gelding over to the woman and dismounted to kneel by her side. He could not see her chest rising or falling, and he thought she had probably been kicked to death. "Miss?"

He gripped her shoulder and started to turn her over but, suddenly, she screamed and thrust a small kitchen knife at his belly. Long Rider just managed to twist his shoulders enough so that the knife only cut a mean gash across the hard muscles of his belly instead of ripping into one of his vitals. She stabbed again, but this time he was ready and grabbed her wrist.

"What the devil is wrong with you!" he shouted, looking down at her with anger and disgust. "I mean you no harm."

The young woman had an angry bruise under her left eye and her lip was swollen. She looked up at Gabe and then her head rolled to one side, and she studied the dead man for a long moment before the tension went out of her body and she whispered, "I'm all right now. You can stop hurting my wrist."

Gabe released the woman and tossed the knife aside. "Was he your husband?"

"He wanted to be," she said, sitting up and touching her lips. "He took me from Cheyenne against my will. He said that he was going to marry me and make me a good woman. I said I liked myself just fine the way I was, and that made him crazy mad. He beat me half to death a week or so ago and he was good at it."

"Couldn't you do something about that?"

"I was fixin' to," she said, brushing back her dark hair from her eyes. "I finally did manage to get ahold of this knife and I was going to use it on him first chance.

But he was careful and I think he knew I would kill him if I could.''

"You from Cheyenne?'' Gabe asked, helping the woman to her feet.

She wore a yellow cotton dress that had once been pretty with white lace around the neckline and cuffs of her sleeves. She was barefoot and dirty and her dark brown hair was tangled with sticks and grass. As Gabe watched, she tried to brush herself clean, but it was hopeless.

"There's a creek back about two miles,'' he said. "You could clean up there.''

"I'd like that. Jeb never let me wash. He didn't much believe in cleanliness. But I can see by the cut of you that you're a different-thinkin' sort of man. My name is Annie Rooney, what's yours?''

Gabe told her and finished by saying, "Before we go anywhere, though, I've got to bury this man. Is there a pick or a shovel in that wagon?''

"There's both. But Jeb don't deserve a burial. He was mean and vicious. His father was a preacher and Jeb couldn't make up his mind if he wanted to be a saint or the devil. Being a saint was too hard and his natural inclination was to be a devil, so that's the way he mostly was. But sometimes, he'd spout words from the Bible so you'd know he had to be the son of a preacher man. He could be mighty self-righteous at times.''

"I'm sorry he got shot,'' Gabe said.

"You did the right thing. You saved me from doin' the job myself, and it would have been a lot harder on him if I'd had to use the knife.''

"Where was he taking you?'' Gabe asked as he found the pick and shovel and walked a little ways off to start working. But first, he pulled off his shirt and inspected the gash she had administered with the kitchen knife.

"Damn, but I'm sorry about that,'' Annie said, looking as if she really meant it. "When he kicked me, I blacked out for a few minutes and the next thing I knew you were turning me over. I thought you were Jeb and you were going to . . . well, you know. He was always wantin' to climb onto me after a beating. He'd get real excited and say he was sorry and everything. The worse the beatin' he'd give, the more excited and sorry he'd be afterward.''

Annie found a rag and used his canteen to wet it before she said, ''Here, let me clean that off.''

''It'll do better to scab if you leave the blood on,'' he told her.

''I'll leave a little blood if you want,'' she said, touching the damp cloth to his stomach and gently cleansing it. ''You sure haven't got an ounce of fat on you, Gabe Conrad. You're a fine-looking man.''

Gabe looked down at her as she worked on his stomach. He had never felt comfortable handling compliments and he was not sure what to say now. ''I best get that man buried,'' he finally mumbled.

Gabe took hold of the pick and began swinging it at the ground, which proved to be riddled with stones. But once he had the grave cut out and worked his way down to about two feet, the ground became softer, and he switched over to the shovel.

''That's plenty deep enough for a man like he was,'' Annie said when the grave was only about three feet deep. ''Just roll him in and cover him up. Way I see it, you done the world a favor by killing him. You sure drilled him dead center.''

Gabe was very tempted to explain that he had not ''drilled'' anyone. But he kept his mouth shut and kept digging until the hole was a respectable depth. ''That ought to be good enough.''

''I hope the coyotes dig him up and eat him,'' she said. ''Jeb like to eat . . . well, he'd eat anything that excited him.''

Annie almost smiled as she turned away for a moment

and her meaning brought a little color to Gabe's cheeks.
He climbed out of the grave and wasted no time in drag-
ging Jeb's body over and dumping it in. Fortunately, it
landed faceup so he didn't have to turn it over. Gabe
was not a superstitious man, but he would not have buried
anyone facedown in the dirt.

"You want to say a few Christian words?"

"Nope," she replied. "He is already in hell if there
is a God."

Gabe thought about his mother's Bible in his saddlebags. If Annie had not been so set against this man he
would have gotten the Bible and read a few words instead
of just shoveling dirt in and tromping it down hard to
keep the critters from digging Jeb up for a midnight meal.
He even replaced the chunks of sod so that the fresh
brown soil did not stand out, telling man and animal
alike that here was a grave.

"You did a good job," Annie said as they walked
away. "Maybe I shouldn't have been so hard on Jeb.
Maybe he just couldn't help being the way he was."

"We all have some good and some bad inside of us,"
Gabe told her. "Sometimes one takes over the other for
a while or even for keeps. I don't know why some men
go bad and stay bad."

Annie looked up at him. "You think real deep and
good, Gabe. I strongly admire a man who can think like
you."

Gabe said, "I'll unhitch the team and you can ride
one of the horses back with me to the creek. There will
be a blacksmith sent along directly to fix the axle and
help get you into Summer Creek."

"Then why don't we just leave the team hitched so
we don't have to hitch 'em back up again?"

"They're your horses now," he said, glancing at a
stout pair of fine draft mares.

"I guess I'll sell them and the wagon along with all
the stuff inside."

"You could do that in Summer Creek or even Rawlins. Ought to get you at least two hundred dollars all together."

"Will you help see I don't get skinned in the deal?"

Gabe nodded. "I'll help."

She smiled and it entirely transformed her face. For the first time he noticed that she had a sunburst of freckles across her cheeks and her eyes were a lovely shade of dark green.

Annie looked happy. "I guess my fortunes have sure turned since you killed Jeb. Here I am with a man I like and admire instead of one I hated. And I got a couple hundred dollars' worth of stuff to sell and nothing but opportunity staring me in the face."

Gabe mounted his sorrel and kicked his boot out of his left stirrup. "Come on up behind me," he said.

Annie had found a clean dress and some other things of hers and stuffed them into a bag, which made it a little difficult climbing up behind him, but she managed with his help. Once in place behind his saddle, she wrapped her arms tightly around his stomach until he grunted with pain.

"I'm sorry! I forgot I knifed you!"

"Just hang on to the cantle and you won't fall off," he said, touching the flanks of his horse with spurs and sending them into an easy gallop.

When they reached the creek, they dismounted and Gabe removed his shirt again and sat down beside a deep pool of water. He yanked off his boots and then smiled. "I'm taking this pool, you can have the next one 'round that bunch of rocks."

"I'd feel a lot safer being close to you," she told him, staying close by his side.

Gabe did not argue. Annie was no blushing virgin and she proved that by undressing right next to him. Gabe shucked off his britches and followed her into the water. She looked very white as she swam around and around in the pool playing and splashing like a girl.

She swam up to him and her eyes were laughing and gay. "Yes, sir, two hours ago I thought life wasn't worth living. Then, like a knight in shining armor, you magically appear and the sun begins to shine and the world looks oh-so-nice!"

Before Gabe could say anything, Annie threw her arms around his neck and kissed him hard. He was standing chest deep in water and when she wrapped her legs around his lean hips he almost fell over backward. She was kissing him so passionately and her hips were pushing at his with such an urgency that he had no doubts that she wanted him right where he stood.

"Do it to me right now," she panted. "Standing right here so tall and proud in this clean, cool water. That's how I want you the first time."

Gabe felt his manhood began to pulsate into a big erection, and Annie must have felt it, too, because she reached down and grabbed him and then opened herself up as wide as she could. "Shove it in all the way," she whispered wetly into his ear. "Hurry!"

Gabe's hands slid down to her firmly rounded buttocks and he took a wet grip on both her spreaded cheeks and then, with the water making his entry smooth, he rocked his hips forward and impaled her.

Her head swayed back and her mouth opened wide. He looked down and saw her eyes rolled up a little, and then she recovered and said, "Oh, you are so big!"

Satisfied that he was going to be a pleasure for her, Gabe slowly began to pump his throbbing penis in and out, and Annie locked her heels and enthusiastically joined his rhythm.

"Don't hurry it," she begged, lifting one of her nice little breasts for him to take in his mouth. "Don't hurry this if it takes all day."

Gabe's lips found her nipple and he began to tease it until it was hard and the woman was squirming mightily and beginning to dig her fingernails into his back. Surging through the water, Gabe struggled toward shore. He knew that he wasn't going to make it before he exploded, so he when he got to knee level, he fell on Annie, who cried out with delight.

"Yes, yes! Do it now!"

Gabe could not have stopped the driving rhythm of his powerful hips if he'd wanted to. Every thrust pushed her soft young body deeper into the mud, but he didn't care and neither did Annie.

Crying out with animal pleasure, Annie lost control of herself, and so did Gabe. Water splashing, mud roiling up all around them, they came together in a slippery, driving orgasm that left them both weak and gasping for breath.

Gabe had to drag Annie up to the shore, and she could not stop grinning. "Where are you going after we get to Summer Creek?"

"I don't know," he said, surprised by her question.

"Then I don't, either," she sighed, "because I am stickin' to you like warts on a toad!"

Gabe laughed outright. But later, when she climbed back on top of him wanting everything he could give, he wasn't so sure that he might like to have her stick close for a while.

CHAPTER SIX

Holly Brown did not tell anyone at Fort York that she was leaving, but Aaron Lydick must have informed Captain Stone. One warm afternoon, the captain tipped his hat and said, "I know that the men on this post, as well as the women, will be sorry to see you leave, Mrs. Brown. You've been a courageous example for everyone."

Holly was not in a chatty mood and had no intention of being charitable. "That's nice to hear. It's a shame, however, that a widow whose husband gave his life to the Army finds herself booted out of her military housing."

The captain expressed surprise and indignation. "Now, Mrs. Brown, that is hardly the case! No one is 'booting' you out of Fort York. It is simply that we have other officers who would like to send for their wives and families. We can't afford to tie up the few houses for married officers."

"And I suppose," Holly said, "that Mr. Lydick reminded you of that fact."

"Mr. Lydick had nothing to do with bringing the matter to my attention."

"I wish I could believe that," Holly said, "but I don't. I believe you made a deal to release Mr. Gabe Conrad just like you made a deal to send me to Summer Creek."

Captain Stone's jaw clenched and he turned and stomped back into the commander's office. Holly did not care that she had angered the man, and when the wagon from Summer Creek arrived the next afternoon she left Fort York without a backward glance.

The driver of the wagon was named Otis Weaver and his wife's name was Edna. They were a friendly old couple, and even though Edna complained about the dust and the long, hard trip over from Summer Creek, she was generally pleasant.

"We came from Missouri," she said. "We had a dry-goods store there for nearly sixteen years. Sold it last month and we're opening a new one in Summer Creek. That town is sure going to grow into something special. With Mr. Lydick's money and good name, it'll be the capital of Wyoming someday."

"That's right," Otis said, nodding his whiskered chin and puffing on his corncob pipe as he drove the wagon along. "The town has plenty of water, it's right next to Mr. Lydick's own railroad, and a mile from the Union Pacific. There's room for everything. You're going to like Summer Creek, ma'am."

"I hope so," Holly said. "I'm going to open a millinery shop."

The pair exchanged glances. "Well," Otis finally drawled. "That's real nice, but seeing as how there are only about a dozen women in Summer Creek, business might be a tad slow for the next few years."

"A dozen?" Holly felt her spirits sink. "Mr. Lydick

led me to believe that there were a good many more than that.''

"Oh, there will be!" Edna said quickly. "Maybe you could think of some other business to sort of take up the slack when things were slow."

Holly tried to hide her troubled thoughts. "I'll survive," she said lamely. "I am a survivor."

"That big china cabinet and four-poster of yours is sure beautiful," Edna said. "I never seen anything nicer."

"Thank you," Holly said. "It's my pride and joy. It was given to my late husband by his grandmother. It came over from Germany fifty or sixty years ago. They are the only nice things I have."

"Well, they must be worth a lot of money. Hand-carved out of some fancy wood," Otis said. "Bet you could get a hundred dollars for each of them."

"Possibly, but they'll never be for sale." Holly turned her attention to the countryside around her and as the Weavers talked, she let her mind drift back to the day of her marriage and then of her honeymoon. There had been good times for her and her husband back in the beginning. Back before gambling had become the most important thing in his life.

Otis and Edna must have had orders because they traveled steadily all that day and did not stop for the night until almost eleven o'clock. They hobbled the horses and ate a cold picnic meal and then collapsed in weariness.

"I'm too damn old for this," Edna whispered when they thought Holly drifted off to sleep. "And I don't care how much he's payin' us, next time I'm staying to home."

"*Shhh*!" Otis hissed. "We owe too much to Mr. Lydick to ever refuse the man. So just go to sleep and we'll be home tomorrow."

"Too damn old and my bones hurt on this hard

ground,'' the old woman groused. "I deserve a straw mattress, at least!''

"Go to sleep!"

Holly stared up at the constellations and thought about what tomorrow would bring. It was encouraging to her that Aaron had been thoughtful enough to provide her with a woman chaperon, even though poor Edna was complaining. Maybe things would be all right in Summer Creek, after all. Certainly, this sweet old couple sure believed in the town's future. And if there were not yet enough women in Summer Creek to make a millinery store profitable, then she would just do something else, though she could not think of what that might be.

Holly drifted off to sleep some time after midnight and awoke at dawn to hear Edna groaning. "My poor old bones are never goin' to be the same again. I'll never walk in my life and—''

"*Shhh*!" Otis hissed angrily. "You'll wake Mrs. Brown up and we got orders to let her sleep in so that—''

Holly opened her eyes. "It's all right," she said. "I'm awake. Here, Mrs. Weaver. Let me help you up and into the wagon.''

"Bless your kindness," the woman said as she struggled to her feet and hobbled over to the wagon, where she had to almost be lifted into the seat. "You are a kind and thoughtful young woman. Mr. Lydick is very fortunate to have a lady friend like you.''

Holly said nothing. She rolled up their bedding while Otis hitched the team. Her few pieces of furniture were still intact, and the bumpy wagon ride did not appear to the hurting them, so she felt relieved.

"Is that beautiful china cabinet and bed ridin' all right? No scratches or anything?'' Edna fretted.

"It's fine," Holly answered, helping Otis water the horses from a leaky bucket before she climbed up to the seat and patted the older woman's hand. "I'm more worried about you than I am about that furniture.''

Edna managed a smile, though she looked very tired. She was a small woman, who, with her husband, must have been in their mid-sixties. "I've just become old and crotchety, dear. I hope you live to enjoy your last years in good health."

Holly wasn't worried about her 'last years.' Mostly she was concerned about what she would find in Summer Creek and how her life would go in the next few days. If she could establish herself as an independent woman, then she'd do fine. But if Aaron intended her to be his public mistress, then her lot in Summer Creek would be bitter indeed.

I have to be respectable, she told herself firmly. I have to be or ladies like Edna will turn their faces away from me and I'll be considered nothing but a kept woman. A well-paid prostitute.

They pulled out as soon as the team was hitched, leaving nothing to mark their overnight stay except that the grass was chewed down close where the two horses had been grazing all night. It was noon before they caught their first look at Summer Creek.

"It's bigger than I expected," Holly said as they came in toward the north end. Far to the south, Holly could see the Union Pacific Railroad tracks and then Aaron's own rails leading north into town and then running straight toward Canada, disappearing into the hills.

"That's Mr. Lydick's mansion down there at the west side of town," Otis said, pointing his finger. "He's mayor and owner all rolled into one."

"Doesn't it bother you to have one man with so much power over your lives?"

The woman shook her head. "We believe in Mr. Lydick. Summer Creek is his town and he's going to take care of it and us. We bought a small dry-goods store and when we aren't runnin' it, our oldest son, James, he's doing everything. James is a fine young man, Mrs.

Brown. He's about your age. I'm going to see that you two are introduced right away.''

For the first time on the long journey, Otis barked at his wife. ''She's spoken for, you old fool! Are you losin' your good senses! She's Mr. Lydick's woman.''

Holly started to protest, to tell them that she was her own woman and that no one owned her, but she decided it would be a waste of breath. This couple obviously placed Aaron on a pedestal. So she just kept quiet and had a good look at Summer Creek.

It was bigger and more attractive than she'd imagined. She was impressed by a big sign posted squarely in the middle of a huge lot that they passed at the south end of town which read: FUTURE SITE OF WYOMING STATE HOUSE AND CAPITOL BUILDING.

''Mr. Lydick is going to get us a state house someday,'' the driver said. ''He said he was, and we believe he will. That's why everything on Lydick Street has to be whitewashed every spring. You'll never see any other town in the West that looks so fine as this.''

A little ways further, Holly saw a water wagon and a sign reading Summer Creek Volunteer Fire Company No. 1. There were the usual shacks and homes on the second and third streets and a few more out to the west of town near the railroad depot and water tower. The main street of town was named Lydick, and even though Holly thought the name was the height of pretentiousness, she was favorably impressed to see more than a dozen shops, saloons, and businesses. Each one was freshly whitewashed and had the outward appearance of prosperity. And on the corners of every street, someone had even planted trees and protected them by building ornamental iron fences around them. Obviously, when one man owned a town and he was trying to promote it, certain amenities were going to be highly visible.

''That's our place right there,'' the woman said, pointing a finger to a small but attractive little store. ''Our house is just one block behind it. It's a nice house, the biggest on Aaron Street.''

''Oh yes, that's the name of it. It's on the better side of town.''

Holly was trying to think of a reply when a handsome young man in his early twenties stepped outside of the dry-goods store and waved, causing Edna to say, ''That's our good-lookin' James. Isn't he a fine-looking young man?''

''Yes,'' Holly said. ''I can see why you're very proud of him.''

The young man stared at Holly with more than casual interest, but she looked straight ahead because she knew that she could only cause him trouble with Aaron Lydick if she encouraged a friendship.

''Ain't we even goin' to stop for a minute so I can climb down?'' Edna crabbed.

''No,'' Otis snapped. ''Our orders were to bring Mrs. Brown straight on in, and that's what we're goin' to do, so sit still and let me do what we was told.''

Edna was stung by the rebuke and their son James looked bewildered as the wagon rolled by him without even pausing to say hello and make quick introductions.

They passed the Elkhorn Saloon, the Wigwam Bar, and a blacksmith shop along with a large general store and several smaller establishments. There was a Chinese laundry that had a full wash line strung out back and three big and steamy washtubs which Holly could see from her vantage point.

''Where is the hotel?'' she asked.

The couple beside her exchanged veiled glances. ''Well, that's next on the drawing boards. Right now, there's just a tent the men pay a dollar a week to live in.''

''I see. Where will I be staying?''

There was a long pause and then Otis said, ''I'm not sure, Mrs. Brown. All Edna and I know is that we're supposed to deliver you to Mr. Lydick's mansion. I guess he's probably got something in mind.''

Holly's temper flared. "He'd certainly better!"

They rode in tense silence the rest of the way through town, and when they came to the mansion, Holly had to admit it was huge and showy. It looked expensive enough to impress the influential men whom Aaron entertained for business purposes. The house was constructed out of red brick and had a wide covered veranda extending around all but the back side. White wooden trim high-lighted the tall windows, and Holly counted ten porch pillars, each beautifully sculpted for effect.

"Well," Otis said, pulling the team to a halt. "We made it."

He was trying to sound gay and happy but there was a false ring to it, and Holly was wondering why when Aaron came striding out to greet them.

"Welcome!" he called, looking as if he had stepped right out of a fashion magazine with his stylish tan suit, white shirt, and hand-painted tie. "Holly, you look won-derful. Mrs. Weaver, I hope the trip was not too stren-uous."

Edna shook her head. "No, sir. It was just fine. A real pleasure."

"Good!" Aaron said, helping Holly down, his hands lingering on her narrow waist. "I have counted the mo-ments until your arrival, my dear. What do you think of Summer Creek?"

"I think it's very attractive. And your mansion is lovely."

He beamed with delight. "I thought you'd be im-pressed. Everyone else who comes here is. And after that dismal Fort York, well, I think you'll agree that you'll be much happier here."

Aaron looked past her for a moment. "Otis?"

"Yes, sir!"

"Why don't you take your wife home to rest. Come

back in a while and bring your son to help you unload Mrs. Brown's furniture. I have a room all cleared out and—''

Holly stepped back. "Now wait a minute!" she said, shaking her head. "I'm not *staying here*."

Aaron feigned confusion. "But, my dear! There isn't anywhere else in town to stay. We intend to build a hotel, but construction won't begin until late fall. I've eight lovely and empty bedrooms for my guests. You'll be most comfortable here."

Holly knew that if she wavered now, any chance at respectability she might have had was lost. "I won't do that."

The Weavers looked at each other uncomfortably. "I think we'll go along," Otis said, "and come back later after you've talked this over."

"No, wait," Holly said. "I want to stay with the Weavers."

"Impossible," Aaron said.

But Holly wasn't listening to him anymore. She hurried over to the wagon to reach up and touch Edna's hand. "I know I'm putting you in a difficult position. But if you let me use one of the empty bedrooms in your home, I'll gladly give you that antique china cabinet you so admire."

The old woman swallowed when her husband roughly elbowed her and said, "This is none of our concern, Edna. Now, you just keep quiet."

"Please," Holly said, her eyes begging. "Mrs. Weaver, woman to woman, you understand the circumstances. You can have the china closet and my thanks."

"All right, it's a deal."

Holly turned around with a bright smile and said to Aaron, "I am most appreciative for your offer of hospitality, but it really wouldn't look proper, and Mrs. Weaver and I have become good friends. I am sure you understand."

Lydick was trapped and he knew it. "Of course not! How foolish of me not to have realized that living here would put you in a compromising position."

Holly touched his arm. "You are so kind, Aaron. When can we discuss the millinery shop? Mrs. Weaver has explained to me that there are not nearly enough women in this town to support a shop devoted to just millinery, but I'm sure we can come up with some other ideas."

Aaron shot Edna a glance that would have melted ice, and then said, "Fine. We can talk over dinner tonight, if you are up to it."

"I will be prepared to receive you at eight," she told him.

After she was helped back into the wagon, Otis was so angry that his knuckles were white as he gripped the reins. "Edna," he grated, "we'll speak of this later, but you know you sure did put us on his wrong side!"

"Otis, you old fool, there are many things that men will never learn, and one of them is that women know they had better stick together in this world or the menfolk will use them like slaves."

Holly said nothing but she had a difficult time to keep from smiling. It had been a big gamble to count on Edna defying her husband's wishes, but Holly had seen steel in the woman from the beginning and plenty of understanding as well.

When Long Rider finally rode in accompanied by Annie Rooney, driving her repaired wagon, he was feeling a little bushed. Annie had taken a powerful liking to him, so much so that she seemed more inclined to make love than to continue on to Summer Creek.

"My goodness!" Annie exclaimed as they turned the corner on Lydick Street, "This is a pretty nice town!"

"Bigger than I'd thought it would be," Gabe said.

The blacksmith who had come out to fix the wagon's

busted axle pointed with pride to the same sign that Holly
had seen earlier that day, and drawled, "Mr. Lydick says
we'll be the first state capital someday and we're all
banking that he's a man of his word. You'll like this
town, Miss Rooney. I hope you might think about staying. We're a little short of women in Summer Creek and
I'd sure like to see a few more pretty young girls like
you settle here."

Annie loved a compliment. "Well, thank you, Mr.
Horner! Thing of it is, I'm not sure what I'd do here to
make a living."

John Horner scratched his jaw thoughtfully. He was
short but very broad across the chest and shoulders, probably about twenty-five years old, and he had a nice smile.
"Oh, I think you'd do all right. You'd probably get
yourself married off in the first month or so, then you
wouldn't have to worry about a thing."

"Is that right!" Annie said, giggling, then winked at
Gabe. "Hear that? Mr. Horner says I'd have callers with
serious intentions."

"He's probably right," Gabe said. It occurred to him
that if men realized what a pistol Annie was when it
came to making love, she'd have men lined up from here
to the Colorado border. "You'd better give that serious
consideration. I'm not a marrying man."

Annie's smile slipped and she said, "Well, that's what
all men say until they meet the right girl. And I just might
be that right girl for you."

Horner butted in. "Miss Rooney, you ought to take
more time about deciding that," he said. "I'd like to
escort you around the town. Sort of help you get acquainted. Afterward, we can go have something to eat
and talk business. Might be, I can give you a fair price
for this team of horses."

"I want to sell the wagon, too," Annie told him. "I'll
only sell them all together. Seems to me that an enter-

prising blacksmith like you could turn a tidy profit on a wagon.''

"I'd have to put in a new axle. The one in there now is just fixed enough to get us to town without much of a load.''

"Fixin' axles is your business.''

"It is,'' he agreed. "But we need to discuss the matter over a nice lunch.''

Annie looked to Gabe, who shrugged his shoulders. "I think that you'd better let him take you to eat. Besides, I've got some business with Aaron Lydick that needs taken care of. I may be pretty busy these next few months, Annie. If you're staying in this town, you need to make some friends.''

It had not been the answer that she had wanted or expected, but Annie was smart enough to know that pouting or acting possessive would only antagonize Long Rider.

She lifted her chin. "Then I *will* accept Mr. Horner's kind offer.''

Gabe was pleased. It wasn't that he didn't want to continue making love with Annie, but at the same time, he knew that he could not afford to lose sight of his real mission, which was to save the buffalo herds and help his Indian people. To do that, he was going to have to play a very clever game with Aaron Lydick, who was highly intelligent and naturally suspicious of everyone.

"Annie,'' he said, reining his sorrel away from the wagon, "I'll be calling on you later.''

"But you don't even know where I'll be staying! Hell, Gabe, *I* don't even know where I'll be staying.''

"I'll find you,'' Gabe said. "All I'll have to do is ask our local blacksmith, isn't that right?''

John Horner grinned. "You got it figured right, Mr. Conrad. So just go about your business and don't worry a thing about Miss Rooney, here. The situation is well in hand.''

Gabe chuckled at that as he rode toward the two-story mansion at the north end of Lydick Street and wondered if he was about to see the lovely Holly Brown once again.

CHAPTER SEVEN

"Cigar?"

Gabe shook his head and looked up from the legal contract that had just been handed to him. "No, thanks."

Lydick closed the lid on his sterling silver cigar box and settled back in his plush office chair as Gabe read the contract that had just been handed to him by the railroad man who had a look of amusement on his face. "So," Lydick mused aloud, "your mother taught you to read from the Bible. How nice."

Gabe said nothing but kept reading. The contract had a lot of big legal terms that were unfamiliar to him, but it seemed fairly straightforward. When Gabe finished, he said, "It looks good, but I'd be stupid to sign a document written by your lawyer. So let's forget about a contract and make sure we understand each other. I'm supposed to smooth things between the Indians and your railroad so there's no trouble."

"And," Lydick said, raising his index finger, "you're to be my chief guide and buffalo hunter."

Gabe frowned. "I have no interest in hunting buffalo for you."

"I know that," Lydick said, "but if I can't locate the northern herds, there's no profit for me, you, or the Indians. You don't even have to do the shooting, just locate the herds for my men."

Gabe knew that he could not refuse. "And in return, you agree to help the reservation Indians get more food, blankets, and better medical attention. Also, I get twenty percent."

"Fifteen! That's what we agreed upon at Fort York."

"Did we?" Gabe frowned. "I don't believe we shook on that or signed anything. I think twenty percent is a rock-bottom figure. Besides, you're not going to send me back to Fort York over five percent."

Lydick used a little gold-plated knife to cut off the tip of his cigar, which he sucked reflectively before he grumbled, "All right. You've got your nerve, but you're right. Why quibble over five percent? We have a deal."

They shook hands across the big desk, and Lydick said, "I'll be in contact with you tomorrow with a couple of men. I'd like you to leave for the northern country right away."

"I'll be going alone," Gabe said. "If I take a bunch of your gunnies, I'll never see an Indian and I won't be able to help you make your unofficial treaty."

Touching a match to the cigar, Lydick said, "That's true, but on the other hand, if you go alone, I may never see you again, and there's no telling what you'll say to Indians. You see, if it hasn't already occurred to you, I trust no one. Especially Indian lovers like you. No offense intended."

Gabe went to the door. "No offense taken. All right, I'll agree to two of your men coming north with me. No more. And they've got to understand that what I say stands without argument. I won't have any little generals, and I know the Indians better than anyone you can send along to watch over me. One stupid word or gesture can easily ruin any chance I'll have to smooth things out for your railroad plans.''

Lydick thought that over for a minute before he dipped his chin. ''Very well.''

The railroad man opened his desk drawer and removed a hundred-dollar bill. ''This is a little advance. You're going to need a pack horse to bring back some jerked buffalo meat, evidence that you are able to find the buffalo. You'll also need supplies and maybe some trinkets or whiskey for the Indians.''

Gabe could scarcely hide his contempt. ''The kind of Indians I'll speak to would be insulted by the offer of whiskey and trinkets. I'll be dealing with leaders, not a bunch of followers and weaklings.''

''Then buy them whatever you think might please them,'' Lydick said with a wave of his hand. ''I leave the matter entirely up to you.''

Gabe took the money and left without another word. On his way out, he peered up and down the hallway but saw no sign that Holly Brown had arrived and moved into Lydick's mansion. She might be upstairs, but he could not hear a sound from anyone, and so he left the house wondering if Holly had arrived from Fort York.

That question was answered only a few minutes later as he rode past a large house and saw Holly sitting on the front porch, reading. Gabe recalled the warning he'd received from Aaron to stay away from Holly, but one look at her and he knew that it was a warning that he would completely ignore. He might have to accommodate the railroad man in ways that he did not like in order to figure out a means to thwart his grand scheme, but Holly Brown was fair and very inviting game.

Gabe dismounted, tied his horse to the neat picket fence and walked up to the porch. ''Hello.''

She looked over her book and rewarded Long Rider with a radiant smile. "Well, if it isn't the famous Long Rider of the Oglala Sioux! So you did go to work for Mr. Lydick despite all your high ideals."

Gabe stepped upon the porch and removed his hat. "Maybe I went to work for Lydick *because* of my ideals."

Her eyes measured his as she said, "Yes, that seems far more likely. But why would you tell me this? You must know that I am also in Aaron's debt."

"I don't know why," Gabe confessed. "But when I saw you sitting here just now and knew that you'd somehow managed to avoid his honeyed net, then I realized that I could trust you."

"Are you always so intuitive in making your decisions?"

"I was raised from a tepee and that word isn't in the Bible. What does 'intuitive' mean?"

"It means, do you often trust your life to total strangers simply on the basis of a hunch or an inner feeling?"

"No," he said. "But I have a notion that you and I are kind of linked up in whatever is going to happen next. I sort of figured that you could use someone to trust and so could I."

Holly thought about it a moment, then placed her book down and stood up to link her arm through Gabe's. "Mr. Conrad, would you be so good as to show me the town?"

"I only just saw it as I rode in."

"Then that makes two of us," Holly said. "Besides, people will see us together, and that will be very helpful to me because I don't want anyone to get the first impression that I am Aaron Lydick's woman."

"I can understand that," Gabe said as he headed for town, wondering if he might bump into someone whom he would not want to meet in Holly's company. Someone like Annie Rooney, for example, who might actually fly into a jealous tantrum at the sight of a beautiful woman on his arm.

But they did not see Annie, much to Gabe's relief. They walked up and down the street, making idle conversation, learning a little bit about each other, and visiting the many shops and stores.

"I came here," Holly said, "prepared not to like Summer Creek. Instead, I am charmed by this quaint but lovely community and I see it as having endless possibilities for growth."

"Then I take it you mean to stay?"

"I might as well," she said. "I have no family, and after living at an Army outpost for the last few years, the prospect of a big city seems a little frightening. I considered going to California, but I don't know anyone there and I do love the Wyoming Territory."

"Then you should stay."

"I know," she said in agreement. "The problem I face is that I can't decide what kind of business I can establish in Summer Creek without becoming hopelessly indebted to Aaron."

"That is a tough decision," Gabe said, "especially given that the man owns this town. Maybe you could start up another laundry."

"No. I don't wish to compete with a nice Chinese family that's already here."

"Then a seamstress. That wouldn't take much more than a needle and thread and maybe some fliers to put about town. Even men can use a little stitch and sewin' work on their clothes. Are you good with a needle and thread?"

"Quite good," she said. "I'll consider that idea. Mrs. Weaver has agreed to introduce me to the ladies, and I may be able to come up with other ideas. Aaron will no doubt have my life planned out by this evening at dinner."

"If you deal with the man, sign nothing," Gabe said.

"I have a feeling that you could be very sorry if he ever felt you disappointed him in any way."

"I'm afraid I've already disappointed him," Holly said with a half-smile, remembering their first encounter. "He had a room all ready for me to move in to when we arrived. He was pretty annoyed when I refused to stay at his mansion."

Gabe said nothing as they walked along the street. When they had made the complete circuit, he said, "I guess we've seen all there is of Summer Creek."

"Why don't we walk down to the railroad junction and see where the rails meet?" she suggested. "There looks to be a pretty stand of trees down there and some cattle pens. I'm not ready to go back to Mrs. Weaver's house yet and it's several hours before I'm supposed to have dinner with Aaron."

"Are you sure?"

"Yes," she said, judging him carefully, "but are you? It seems to me you have more to lose than I if Aaron is upset about us being together."

Gabe had to agree. It wasn't that he worried about any reprisals from the jealous railroad man—and he had been warned to avoid her—it was just that he did not want to jeopardize the opportunity to learn how to stop Lydick before he succeeded with his greedy plans to slaughter the buffalo.

"I'm sorry," she said. "I see that I've placed you in a difficult, perhaps even dangerous, position."

"The hell with that," Gabe said. "I feel like taking a walk, too."

They followed Lydick's railroad tracks south toward the tracks of the Union Pacific. As they grew nearer, they could see the details of the water tower, the cottonwood trees which were fed by a windmill, and the large collection of stock pens and loading chutes where the tracks met.

"Do you know what Lydick intends to do up north?"

Gabe asked when they stopped to rest on a grassy place in the shade of the cottonwood trees.

"I think so. He wants to slaughter the buffalo herds and also swindle a bunch of poor emigrants. Isn't that it?"

"Yeah. That sums it up pretty close. I hope to stop him."

"You can't. He's got all the hole cards, including the politicians and the United States Army. He's a man that doesn't miss a bet. The only thing you can do is to try and help the Indians get something out of it for their buffalo. I assume that's your plan."

"That's right," Gabe said. "But I'll tell you a secret. I won't sit back and let him have his way with the buffalo herds. If I have to, I can at least make things pretty rough for his hunters."

"You shouldn't be thinking that way," she said. "You'll only wind up getting shot on the plains. Have you met Wyatt Noonan yet?"

"No. Who is he?"

There was a water tank fed by the windmill's pump and Holly dipped her hands into the water and bathed her face. "It feels wonderful," she said before explaining. "Wyatt Noonan is Aaron's top enforcer. He is also a famed marksman and buffalo hunter. I have seen him in shooting matches and he cannot be beat. He uses the same kind of rifle that Aaron uses. A beautiful hunting rifle with a Swiss scope."

Gabe thought back to how that rifle had blown a fist-sized hole through Jeb's chest and how easy Aaron had made the shot appear with his fancy custom hunting rifle. "I saw it," Gabe said without elaboration. "That is quite a rifle."

"There is nothing short of artillery that can match it for long-distance accuracy and firepower. You'd stand no chance against Noonan, and I have never seen a man that scared me the way he does. What I am saying, Gabe, is that such a man will kill you for sure if you cross him—or his boss. I don't want that to happen.''

Gabe rolled over onto one elbow and studied the young woman whose face was less than a foot away from his own. "Why do you care? We're almost strangers."

"I know, but somehow we seem to have a common destiny. I mean, we are both struggling to outwit and survive against Aaron and it all seems so hopeless.''

Gabe reached out and pulled the woman close. He kissed her lips and she did not pull away from him. "It isn't at all hopeless.''

"It isn't?'' Using his arm as a pillow, Holly gazed up at the sky and the clouds. "Oh, but I'd so love to believe it when you say that!''

"Then all you have to do is imagine that we will win, and I'll do the rest. I promise,'' Gabe said, wanting to kiss her and make love to her but sensing that this was not the time or the place.

"What I can imagine is how this country must have seemed before the white man came. Before the railroad was here, or the Army, or anyone but the Indian. I don't suppose you saw it that way.''

Gabe flopped over on his back. "No, it was before my time. You see, I was conceived only a few minutes before my father was killed by Indians as they were trying to reach the Black Hills. My mother was taken and she wanted to die for a long time but grew to love the Indian way so much she could not return to the white man's world.''

"But you did.''

"Yes,'' Long Rider said. "I was sent away from the Indian people by my mother, who pretended she did not want me any longer. The man who took me, and whose name I bear, was Jim Bridger—better known as Old Gabe. He was a good man, and only later did I discover that he did what he had been asked.''

"But why?''

Gabe took a deep breath and let it out slowly, for the memory of how his mother had pretended to send him away still hurt after all these years, even though he now understood her motives. "My mother could see into the future. She had visions and she knew that the good days of the Indians were past. That the Army and the whites would soon take our lands by force and herd us onto reservations like so many cattle. She did not want that for me and decided that I could not stay among the Oglala if I was ever to be free."

Holly turned to him. "Is it so terrible living among us whites?"

"No," he said quickly. "There are things that are very good, and things very bad. It is just different and sometimes . . . sometimes I feel as if I am being pulled apart. I am white, but I am also Oglala Sioux."

She brushed his cheek with her cool fingertips. "I can't even imagine how it must seem," she confessed. "I knew the first time that I saw you that you were unique and very special. I was immediately attracted to you for that reason."

"I am just a man. You know men."

"Yes," she said, her eyes dropping to his chest. "It has been a long time for me without a man. My husband and I enjoyed our nights together very much."

Long Rider touched the front of her dress, where it was gathered up in a mound over her bosom. Holly edged closer. "We can't do this," she said. "Not now or like this."

He rubbed her breast a little harder and she sighed with satisfaction. "Why not?"

"Because I've already stayed too long and—"

Gabe turned to hear the sound of hoofbeats, and when he saw riders galloping alongside of a carriage, he stood up fast.

"Oh, my God!" Holly whispered. "It's Aaron and

Noonan. Gabe, please don't say a word. If you do, it will cause even more trouble.''

Gabe stared at the rapidly approaching men. "I'd guess the one on the flashy palomino is Wyatt Noonan.''

"Yes.''

"Is he an expert with a handgun?''

Holly nodded. She was suddenly pale with fear.

"So am I,'' Gabe said, touching the butt of his Colt. "And stop worrying. Nothing so bad will happen to either of us. Not as long as Aaron needs us for his own purposes.''

"You're right,'' Holly said. "But that still doesn't stop my hands from shaking.''

Gabe had seen men like Wyatt Noonan before. The buffalo hunter, marksman, and gunslinger was his own age and size, only he wore grease- and blood-crusted buckskins and a raccoon-skin cap instead of a Stetson. Noonan looked imposing, with a three-day growth of spiky black whiskers and a Colt tied down snugly to his powerful right thigh.

The other man was smallish but equally dangerous looking. He was dressed in fancy clothes and wore a stitched leather vest decorated with silver conchos. He had a pearl-handled six-gun riding high on his hip and a wispy moustache and goatee.

"Who's the other gunman?'' Gabe asked as they drew near.

"Purvis Monk,'' she said. "He's said to be a back-shooter.''

"It figures.''

The carriage and two outriders drew up and Aaron looked furious. "Mrs. Brown,'' he hissed, "we have a dinner date and I've come to escort you back to Summer Creek.''

"We were just about to start back,'' she said.

"Good! Then I'll save you the trouble of walking. Get in, please.''

Holly looked at the other two men. "What about Mr. Conrad?"

"He is leaving tomorrow with Wyatt and Purvis. They need to talk things over and I thought this was as good a time as any."

"But—"

"Get in!" Aaron repeated, his voice taking on a steely edge.

"Do as he says," Long Rider told the woman. "I'll be fine."

"Are you sure?"

Gabe did not take his eyes off the two hired gunmen. "Yes. Get in the carriage, Holly. Enjoy your dinner, but remember what I said."

"What *did* you say?" Aaron demanded.

Gabe did not bat an eye when he replied, "I told her not to sign any contracts with you."

Aaron's mouth crimped at the corners. "You are in no position to advise others, especially when it comes to dealing with me. Holly?"

Holly climbed into the carriage and Aaron said to his men, "I'm sure you have plenty to talk over with Gabe. If I don't see you before you go north early tomorrow morning, I trust you'll find a way to keep me well informed."

Wyatt and Purvis nodded grimly as their boss turned the carriage around and drove Holly back to Summer Creek.

"Well," Gabe said, his hands close to his gun butt. "Are you boys going to fish or cut bait?"

Noonan climbed down from his horse. He was even taller than Gabe but it was now apparent that he was a few hard years older. "I was ordered to teach you a lesson in how to take orders," he said. "But I'm not supposed to kill you, so you're real lucky."

Noonan unbuckled his gun belt. "You man enough to take your medicine?"

"I sure am," Gabe said, leaving his gun belt on and motioning Noonan to come in closer.

Noonan wore moccasins and he came in fast. Gabe ducked a whistling right hand and buried his own left into the man's side. Noonan staggered and when Gabe hit him again, the man dropped to one knee and somehow administered a vicious sweep kick, catching Gabe just above the ankles and bringing him crashing to earth.

Noonan was on him like a big catamount. They locked and rolled over and over, punching and gouging, grunting and choking. Noonan was bear-strong but Gabe was a shade quicker, and he delivered three punches for every two that were hammering his face. He was doing fine, though, and when he finally got astraddle the man's chest, he might even have finished the fight, except that Purvis had jumped for his horse with his Winchester rifle and brought its barrel slashing down toward Gabe's skull as if it were an ax.

Gabe didn't even see the blow because he was fighting to stay on top and win. One instant he was planting his fist in Noonan's whiskers, the next he was dropping down a dark hole.

CHAPTER EIGHT

Holly studied the rich man from across the dining-room table. They were in a small, private alcove of a surprisingly elegant restaurant. Their table was graced by crystal goblets filled with white wine. Silver candelabra matched the table service. However, despite their surroundings, there had been a strain between them since Aaron had rudely ordered her into his carriage and driven her away from Long Rider.

Aaron lit a cigar and puffed a few moments before saying, "How did you like the seafood dinner, my dear? I had it shipped on ice all the way from the California coast."

"It was wonderful," she said, grateful that he had at last broken the strained silence. "I've never had anything so delicious. Out here on the frontier, about all you can get is chicken, beef, or wild game."

"I know. That's why I so enjoy the novelty of seafood. Prawns, scallops, and clams baked on a half shell.

Shrimp and halibut steaks, they are wonderful served with a chilled white wine from California. Don't you agree?''

"Yes, I do.''

He sighed. "Holly, I must tell you how disappointed I was to see you and Gabe Conrad lying together. Frankly, I was shocked and dismayed. I thought better of you, though I expected that a man raised by savages would have no honor in the company of a lady.''

Holly's cheeks colored. "That's not true!''

"Yes, it is.''

Since he had brought the subject up, she plunged into him as mad as a wet cat. "And you had no right to order me into your carriage as if I were some foot servant or slave! And what did those gunmen of yours do to poor Gabe? Murder him because he dared to ask me to go walking?''

"You weren't walking when I saw you together,'' Aaron said coldly. "And I had warned him to stay away from you. He can have the attentions of any other woman in Summer Creek. So what does he do the moment he leaves my office? He goes to see you.''

Aaron's voice trembled with anger. "I tell you this, if it happens again, he is a dead man.''

Holly pushed to her feet. "I don't have to listen to this! And I don't have to—''

"Sit down!''

Holly found herself unable to stand and so she obeyed his order.

"Now,'' he said, "let's talk about us. You need me and I want you. It's as simple as that.''

She took her wineglass and drank deeply. She needed to regain some of her earlier composure. "Is it?''

"Of course.'' He lowered his voice. "I am prepared to help you become established in any business that you choose to start in return for certain favors.''

Holly swallowed noisily. "I don't think I need to ask

you what 'favors' you are referring to. Aaron, I refuse to give them.''

Aaron pretended not to hear a word she had said and continued on as if he were reciting a well-rehearsed speech. "In return for your favors and in addition to helping you, I will also promise that no harm will come to Gabe Conrad and that he will be allowed to help his Sioux people. I'll even see that they are given a few buffalo that they can breed for themselves so that future generations of Indians will at least be able to see what their ancestors hunted.''

Aaron refilled her glass. "I don't want to be brutish or forceful, Holly. But I *will* have my way in this. You can't oppose me, and Long Rider can't, either. So you can either enjoy my attentions and go first-class for once in your life while at the same time establishing your own profitable business, or you can refuse and I'll see that you are placed on the next train leaving Wyoming.''

She studied the wine in her glass and thought about what he had just said. Tears welled up in her eyes as she felt him take her hand and squeeze it tenderly. "My dear woman, use your head!" he pleaded. "I'm offering you everything. You can have money, respectability—"

"Respectability? How?''

"You can continue to live at the Weavers. We can meet here and at night, where we will not be seen.''

"I don't believe that for a moment. And this thing about Long Rider. You're actually threatening to kill him if I don't agree to your wishes. How can you do that?''

"I won't kill the man—Noonan or Purvis Monk will.''

Holly shivered. "All right,'' she said, expelling a deep breath. "I have no choice.''

"Of course you do! There's a Union Pacific train coming through tomorrow afternoon bound for Omaha, and another rolling by the following morning on its way to Reno and then Sacramento, California. You've got a ticket if you want it. Just say the word and I'll walk out of your life forever.''

And Gabe will soon be dead and so will the buffalo, she thought. "Aaron, I want a thousand dollars in seed money. I've talked it over with Mrs. Weaver and this town needs a newspaper, and I want to be its editor. But it's going to take a printing press, paper, and a lot of other things.''

"A newspaper?" His eyebrows shot up. "Women don't become editors!"

"My father was an editor. I helped him put out a paper in Illinois until I was almost fifteen. I can run a paper and that's what I want to do.''

It was clear that Aaron Lydick had been thrown off balance by this unexpected request. Holly took heart at his momentary confusion and indecision. "Well?"

He steepled his fingertips and began tapping them together. "I have thought we needed a newspaper. A town is not really accorded legitimacy until it has a hotel and a newspaper. But a woman editor? I just don't know.''

"I can do it," she insisted. "But I won't be told what to print, Aaron. I'll print the truth and there might be times when you'll be angry with me,''

"Yes," he said, looking into her uncompromising green eyes. "I'm sure I will. Why can't you think of something more conventional?''

"Because I am not interested in being conventional. Not if I am being coerced into becoming your mistress.''

He smoked thoughtfully for several minutes before he said, "You win. A thousand dollars and no interference in your newspaper. Have we an agreement?''

"Yes!"

He lifted his own glass. "To us," he said, studying her lovely face. "To your paper and our new relationship. May both be infinitely pleasurable and successful.''

Holly's crystal goblet tinkled much more gaily than she felt inside. But she had realized right from the start that she would eventually have to compromise herself if she meant to get what she wanted. At first, she'd thought that she wanted the respectability of his name in marriage. But she had just realized that she could not marry a man who threatened murder. So she'd taken his money and his promises.

"Shall we go? My carriage is waiting just out in the back alley. No one will see you coming to my mansion or leaving."

Holly stood up. She felt a little giddy from the wine and the irrevocable decision she'd just made. A decision that would set her up in business as well as save Long Rider's life. She had sold herself well. "I'm ready."

"Good!"

He came around and took her arm and they went out the back into the alley, where a man stood holding the carriage horse. Aaron assisted her into the carriage and Holly could not help but ask, "How long would you have kept this carriage and that man waiting outside for us?"

"All night if that was what it would have taken," Aaron said as the carriage pulled away and the curtains were drawn.

The carriage delivered them to the back door of the mansion and they wasted no time in going upstairs to Aaron's bedroom. He had a huge four-poster bed that put Holly's treasured bed to shame. He undressed quickly and climbed under the covers to watch her. Feeling his eyes upon her, Holly walked over to the kerosene lamp and blew it out before she pulled the last of her clothes off and stood shivering with a mixture of fear and dread.

As if sensing her resolve crumbling as the very foot of his bed, Aaron lit a candle and, his eyes taking in every inch of her body, he said, "As you are about to find out, I am a very skilled lover, my dear. Come here now! I've already waited much too long."

Before she changed her mind, Holly came to him in

a rush. He was ready for her and when his smooth, soft hands slid down over her breasts and found her hidden treasure, she gasped as he slipped his finger into her and began to excite her beyond all expectations with his long, perfectly manicured fingernail. She had not dared even think about what she would do when he had her in his bed, but certainly she had not supposed she would find herself squirming with pleasure.

"Yes!" he whispered, his tongue laving her nipples. "Enjoy this, Holly. The moment I saw you I knew that you were meant to be my woman. To have me deep inside of you."

Holly moaned and tried to stop her hips from rotating around his finger. But she was powerless and her chest was heaving like a bellows. Moments later, when her heels were sliding back and forth against his incredibly smooth silk sheets, she was kissing him and reaching for his manhood.

"Hurry," she whispered without shame. "I haven't had a man in so long!"

Aaron laughed deep in his chest. "I know that and also how every man at Fort York dreamed of doing this to you. Dreamed of rising up over you and driving his cock into you right to the hilt. Like this!"

Holly cried out with pleasure as he buried himself into her womanhood. He was laving her nipples and driving in and out of her, and she clung to him desperately, trying not to think about how good it felt and how she should be at least holding something back.

But she couldn't hold anything back and when she lost control of herself and began to whimper and thrash under his body, he laughed out loud and slammed his hips harder into hers until he filled her completely with his seed.

Long Rider clenched his teeth and stifled a moan as pain and awareness flooded his mind. When he tried to reach for the rifle butt that was banging him in the face, he realized he was tied both hand and foot.

Gabe raised his head to find that there was a dried river of blood running from a place just above his ear down to his chin.

Purvis Monk reached out and grabbed Long Rider by the hair, yanked his head up, and looked into his pain-wracked eyes before letting go and declaring, "He's finally woke up, Wyatt."

"I see that," the big hunter grumbled. "Let the son of a bitch think about his next move for a couple of minutes."

Gabe hissed, "You better untie me or I'm going to tear your head off when I get loose."

"Then maybe I should kill you," Wyatt Noonan said conversationally. "I got orders from Mr. Lydick not to unless I hear different. But hell, a man has got to think of his own hide."

"I think we *should* kill him," Purvis Monk argued. "We can tell Mr. Lydick he fell off his horse and broke his damn neck."

"Hellfire," Noonan swore, "he'd never believe that. We'd have to think of somethin' a lot better. This man is supposed to help Mr. Lydick. If we kill him, we got to have a damn good reason or we're in deep trouble."

"I'll think on it some," Purvis grumbled. "But he was kickin' your head in when I bashed him with the barrel of my rifle. I never saw you take a whippin' before."

"I wasn't gettin' whipped! I was just gettin' ready to bite off his ear for a snack, and then I was going to roll him over and cut his balls off!"

"Sure," Purvis said with a sneer. "After he'd flattened your face."

"Shut up," Noonan warned, "or I'll wring your scrawny neck like I would a chicken's."

The horses came to a halt and Gabe felt Noonan cut

the bindings from around his ankles and say, "I'm leavin' the ones on around your wrists until we camp tonight. That way, we can talk nice and easy without you stirrin' up a fuss."

"What's there to talk about?" Gabe asked as he dropped down to his feet and steadied himself against the sweaty flanks of his sorrel gelding.

They stood eye to eye and Gabe at least had the satisfaction of seeing that Noonan's lips were broken and his right eye was nearly swollen shut. "I'm supposed to be the man in charge," he said. "That was the deal I made with Lydick."

"Well," Noonan drawled, "he ain't here with us, so piss on that poor deal. I don't trust you and neither does Purvis. We're going to keep your six-gun, but you can keep the Winchester in its boot unless there's Indian trouble. If you play it straight with us, we'll get along fine. But if you mess up or try to sell us out to the Indians, so help me, I'll drill you quicker'n I would a frothin'-at-the-mouth polecat. You understand me plain?"

"I do."

"Good!" Noonan said. "Now, climb back aboard that horse of yours and let's cover some ground. We got to find a couple buffalo and some Indians who can make us a railroad treaty."

Gabe gripped his saddle horn with both hands and pulled himself back into the saddle. He thought about Holly and about Annie and about how bad his head ached and his ears still rang. But he'd mend soon enough to deal with this pair when the time for action came.

"I hear they call you Long Rider," Purvis Monk said meanly.

"That's right."

"Well," Purvis drawled, "they're going to call you 'history' if you try and fuck around with Wyatt or me. We'd as soon ventilate as look at you."

"So I figured," Gabe said.

"Good. Just as long as you know where you stand in our book, we'll get along just fine."

Gabe clenched his teeth and said nothing more as their horses trotted north toward the distant Indian and buffalo country of his youth. He knew the score and he knew that he would probably have to kill Purvis and Wyatt before he returned to Summer Creek—if he returned.

CHAPTER NINE

Annie Rooney was very, very upset. She had heard about Gabe Conrad and Holly Brown parading around Summer Creek as bold as brass and it had damn near broke her heart. And if that wasn't enough to make a poor girl cry, there was the additional news that the rich man and two of his gunslingers had gone hell-bent for leather after Gabe and the new woman in town named Holly Brown that everyone was talking about.

Annie looked at young John Horner, Summer Creek's blacksmith, and said, "I thank you for buying my wagon and horses. Now, I'll have to trouble you for a good saddle horse and outfit."

"Why?"

Annie scuffed the barnyard dirt with the tip of her shoe. "Well, I guess you heard about Long Rider and that Mrs. Brown that went walkin' down to the railroad junction yesterday."

"I did." Horner grinned. "I guess everyone in town

has heard about it as well. Mr. Lydick must be madder than hell. I think he is pretty sweet on that woman, and the first thing she does is go walking with another man. One that was raised as an Indian and probably is no gentleman.''

Annie did not comment on his disparaging remark but asked, ''Did you hear what happened afterward?''

''Sure,'' Horner said, shaping a horseshoe around the horn of his anvil. ''Mr. Lydick drove the Brown woman back to town.''

''But what happened to Gabe?!''

The blacksmith beat at the shoe for a moment, then stopped and held it up to the sky for closer inspection. ''I don't know for sure. But since the two men that went after him along with Mr. Lydick were Wyatt Noonan and Purvis Monk, I'd suspect that they might have killed Gabe outright.''

Annie's face paled. ''But I love him! And he loves me!''

''No, he don't,'' Horner said, dropping the smoking horseshoe into water, where it boiled and sizzled for an instant until it was cool. ''Annie, if he loved you, he wouldn't have gone walking with the Brown woman.''

''Well, he might have! Maybe they were old friends or something.''

Horner scowled. ''I guess you haven't seen what she looks like.''

Annie fretted. ''Pretty, huh?''

''She's a real beauty,'' the blacksmith said, then quickly added, ''but not my type. Altogether too showy for me. I like a plain, simple girl like you.''

Annie did not know whether she should feel flattered or insulted but she was too worried to give it much thought. ''I got to go out there and see if they left Gabe for dead or took him somewheres.''

The blacksmith had been about to shoe a horse, but now he could see that Annie was serious. ''Listen, I'll saddle up a couple of my horses and we'll ride out together just to take a look-see. But if Conrad is gone and we don't find any signs of blood or a fresh-dug grave, you just forget about that man. Odds are he just rode away or was run off by Monk and Noonan.''

"Uh-uh," Annie said. "He would never do that without seeing me first."

"He would if he was shot or run off at the point of a gun."

Annie bit her lip. "Let's hurry and find out. Okay?"

Horner untied his leather apron and washed his rough hands in the tub of water. He fished out the horseshoe and tacked it onto the animal standing close by. Next, he nipped off the tips of the horseshoe nails that he had driven through the hoof, rasped them down smooth, and studied the fit.

"All right, I'll pull the other three old ones and replace them when we get back. The saddles are right over there on the racks. We'll use the two closest to me. Blankets and bridles are on top."

Annie smiled with relief. "Thank you very much. You're a good man, John Horner."

"If Mr. Lydick suspected that I was butting into his affairs like this, I'd be run out of business."

"He could do that?"

"Sure, he could," Horner said, handing Annie a bridle and taking one himself as he got a second horse to ride. "He owns everything here, including the ground that this stable and shop sits on. I got a lease, but he'd find some way to break it and send me packing. His lawyer wrote the damn thing, so that wouldn't be hard."

They saddled the horses quickly and rode out of town going north until they were beyond some low hills. "We can loop around to the south now," Horner said. "I just didn't want anyone to see where we were headed. Summer Creek is a small town and it doesn't take much to stir up a bunch of gossip."

"I'd figure that Gabe and that Brown woman have already given them enough to talk about for about a week," Holly said.

"Some people are always looking for new gossip," Horner said. "They feed on it like flies on . . . well, never mind."

When they reached the Union Pacific stockyards and water tank, they dismounted and studied the tracks. It was easy to see where Lydick's carriage had stopped, and they had no trouble discovering that a scuffle had taken place. Annie found a few drops of darkly stained earth and that worried her enough to send her scurrying about in an ever-widening circle, looking for an unmarked grave.

"I don't see any fresh-dug dirt," she said when she'd covered better than an acre.

"Well, they sure didn't exchange pleasantries out here," Horner said, his blue eyes following the track to the northwest. "Three horses going away. I'll bet they had a fight, settled their differences, and just decided to ride off together like friends."

Annie climbed back onto her horse. "Don't be stupid," she snapped. "Gabe would never become friends with the likes of that pair!"

"Why don't you ask that Brown woman what happened out here before you go racing off into the sunset, probably to get yourself scalped or outraged."

"That's such a damn good idea," Annie said, "that I don't know why I didn't think of it myself."

Annie held on to that idea all the way back to Summer Creek, and as soon as she left the blacksmith, she headed straight off to find Holly Brown. It took her less than five minutes to learn where the woman was boarding. Not one to hang back when she'd set her course, Annie marched right up to the door and banged until Otis Weaver clomped down the hallway to see who was causing all the commotion.

"I come to speak to Miss Brown," Annie said. "And I need to speak with her right away."

"She's resting." Otis glanced over his shoulder and he appeared very displeased. "She was up all hours of the night, but I guess you can go knock on her door. It'd serve her right."

Annie let herself in and tromped down the hall hearing Otis yell, "Second door on the left is hers. Bang it good."

Annie did bang the door pretty loudly and finally her effort was rewarded by the sound of the door's lock turning. When Holly peeked around the corner of the door and saw the young woman, she said in a strained voice, "I'd rather not have company, miss."

Annie stared at the woman. It was clear that she had been up most of the night because her eyes were red and her face was puffy from lack of sleep, and maybe it was bruised, especially around the mouth. Anyone could see that Holly was normally a real beauty, but not this morning.

"Who are you?"

Annie told her and then said, "I was just out to the railroad junction and I found bloodstains on the dirt. I want to know what happened to Gabe Conrad. You *must* tell me."

Holly shook her head to clear away the cobwebs. She did not even want to think about what had happened to her during the last twelve hours. "Miss Rooney," she said, opening the crack wider and seeing Otis staring at her with disapproval, "why don't you come in and sit down while I pull myself together enough to assure you that Gabe Conrad is safe and unharmed."

Annie came inside. The moment she closed the door behind her, she blurted, "How can you be sure?"

"Because," Holly said, "I made Aaron promise me that he would not be harmed."

Annie blinked. She did not need to be told what this

woman had done in exchange for that promise. Holly was probably a sight better off than Annie was, but she was not a wealthy or influential woman. That meant she only had one bargaining chip—the same one that any beautiful woman had to offer. "I . . . I see," Annie said lamely. "I didn't mean to pry."

"Don't worry about it," Holly said. "I'm sure that the news will soon be all over town that I've had two men in the space of one day after my arrival in this town. I must have been a fool to think that I could masquerade as a lady."

Annie did not quite know what to say. She had not expected the woman to be so openly harsh with herself. "Sometimes," Annie said slowly, "we have to do things we don't want to do. And as often as not, no one understands that except ourselves. The Lord said, 'Judge not lest ye be judged.' I guess all of us ought to try a little harder to live by those words."

Holly looked up and tears blurred her vision. "I'm a kept woman now," she said in a dead voice. "I sold my virtue and respect for money, but also to keep Gabe Conrad from being killed. You have to believe the last part."

"I do," Annie said. "And instead of rushing off to find Gabe, I'll just wait here in Summer Creek and hope for the best. I can see that there is no way I could take a man from you."

Before Holly could argue that point, Annie left the room and headed back down the hallway. She passed Otis without meeting his eye or saying a word to him and went straight to the blacksmith's shop, where John Horner was waiting.

"Well," he asked, "what did you find out?"

"I found out that Gabe is safe for now, but that Miss Brown is in bad need of a friend in this town."

"She'll be an outcast among the ladies," Horner said.

"I know." Annie looked up and managed a weak

smile. "But then, I never was a lady, anyway."

"So what are you going to do in Summer Creek?"

"Find work."

Horner wiped his hands on his apron and placed them on Annie's shoulders. "Look," he said. "I know you got strong feelings for this Gabe Conrad fella and I figure you and he, well . . . you got to know each other pretty good before I arrived to fix that busted axle."

When Annie didn't protest or even look up into his eyes, the blacksmith continued. "That don't matter none to me because you didn't even know I existed. I got strong feelings for you, Annie. I got 'em the moment I saw you standing beside your poor old wagon. Those feelin's ain't changed a mite."

"John," she said quietly, "I don't think this is the time or—"

"I may not have the nerve even if there does come a better time," he argued, brushing aside her protest. "And the thing of it is that I may not own the land this barn rests upon, but I own everything else you see. The barn and corrals, the wagons, the anvil and bellows, and the tools. I also own ten head of good horses and four good mules. Altogether, I'm probably worth a thousand dollars of any man's money, and that ain't so bad for being only twenty-six years old. Now is it?"

"No, it isn't," she told him, impressed by the figure.

"Well, see there!" he crowed proudly, "I *am* a man of some means. And I got a good strong back and an even stronger business. I could take you for a wife and support you just fine. It wouldn't be fancy for a few years, but neither of us are fancy people. We could have children and—"

Annie put her fingers across his lips to silence the outpouring of his words. "I'll think on it," she said, trying to offer as much encouragement as she could. "I don't know my left from my right about now, and my head is all mixed up. But I'll stick around and find work and we'll get to know each other better. You might change your mind if you knew all the things that I've done and that's been done to me.''

"That's all in the past. I ain't no saint myself. But together, we'd be a damn good team to pull a fair-sized load down the road of life.''

Annie laughed all of a sudden. "Why, John Horner, I do declare. You got a poetic streak! That 'road of life' stuff was real pretty!''

"You think so?"

"I sure do." Annie kissed his cheek. "I got to find me a place to stay and to work. You come callin' around sunset, hear me?''

The stocky blacksmith fingered his dirty cheek where her lips had brushed his skin. "I guess you don't want to clean stalls or learn to trim a horse's feet?''

"Hell, no!" she called back to him. "I'm no lady, but I'm no man, either.''

John Horner watched her trim little bottom sashay down the road and he said with a grin, "That's for damn sure!''

CHAPTER TEN

Long Rider was led by Wyatt Noonan and Purvis Monk across the Sweetwater River, and then Gabe angled east and hugged the flanks of the Big Horn Mountains, still moving north. They came to the south fork of the Powder River and followed it about thirty miles before leaving it to soon ford Crazy Woman Creek. They were looking for sign of buffalo or hostile Indians and were also scouting the best route for Lydick's railroad.

To Long Rider's way of thinking, this was God's country. The grass was higher than he had ever seen it, and the deer and antelope were fat and as plentiful as jackrabbits. Gabe saw coyotes and even wolves chasing down the weakest game, and it made him sad to think of the ill-fed and -clothed Indian people confined to reservations while this empty land teemed with such abundance.

In the days since leaving Summer Creek, Long Rider had established his leadership despite the fact that he was not allowed to carry his six-gun. On two occasions, he had pulled his Winchester and shot the fast, elusive antelope while Noonan was still fiddling with his telescopic sight. The two gunslingers now understood that, while a fancy high-powered rifle might be more accurate across a long distance, it was also cumbersome and slow enough to get a man killed.

"How far north are we goin' to have to go to find the damn buffalo?" Purvis Monk asked for about the hundredth time.

"I don't know," Gabe said. "Maybe all the way up into Montana. Maybe right up ahead. Used to be, they were thick in this part of the country."

Wyatt Noonan shaded his eyes. "The buffalo hunters must have already been through here a few years back and wiped out the herds."

Gabe said nothing. True, there had been a number of buffalo hunters through this country, but they had been few and far between because this was too far north for the Army to offer them any protection from the Indians. Gabe figured the Indians had been hunting the buffalo and driving them ever farther to the north and out of reach of the white men. Supposedly, the Indians were all "pacified," that being the term the United States Army liked to use. But this was a big and a lonesome country, and there were large numbers of warriors who had refused to live on the reservation.

The Army called these free-roaming Indians "hostiles." These were the last true warriors. Sioux, Crow, a smattering of Cheyenne, and even some Blackfeet who had taken refuge in the Big Horns and other places where they were damn near impossible to find, much less capture. They still lived in the old ways and they had no compunction whatsoever when it came to scalping a hunter who slaughtered their buffalo.

It was high noon on the day that Gabe saw where the grass bent by a dozen or so mounted horses. You could tell when a horse was mounted because it traveled in a straight line instead of meandering here or there like grazing wild horses. To Gabe's surprise, both Wyatt and Purvis missed the signs. Gabe said nothing. He simply became even more alert than normal and his gray eyes moved constantly. The Indians might be friendly or they might be very much the opposite; only time would tell.

The next afternoon they were skirting a pine forest and riding though heavy rocks when Wyatt Noonan suddenly threw his hand up and said, "Hold it!"

Gabe reined his horse to a standstill and twisted around in his saddle. "What's wrong?"

"Indians," Wyatt said, pointing just a ways off to their left. "I see tracks over there."

Gabe had seen the tracks miles back and he knew they were less than a day behind the Indians. "Where?"

"Goddamnit!" Noonan swore with disgust as he galloped over to the tracks. "Right here on these rocks. Some Indian hunter you turned out to be, Long Rider!"

Gabe acted surprised. "I guess they are Indian ponies."

"What are we going to do?" Purvis asked, licking his thin lips. "I sure would rather hunt the buffalo than fuck around with the Indians."

Gabe said, "I thought that Mr. Lydick's main objective was for me to establish some kind of deal with the Indians up in this country so that he could build his railroad in peace. I can't make a treaty without finding them."

Noonan's eyebrows knit with worry. "You're an Oglala Sioux, that right?"

"Yep."

"The Sioux hate the Crow and vice versa. They don't like Blackfeet, either. What if these Indians are Crow or Blackfeet?"

"Then I don't tell them who I am," Gabe said, making light of the complication. "That seems pretty obvious.

They still might deal with your boss if the idea is presented right.''

Monk and Noonan exchanged skeptical glances and when Noonan turned back toward Gabe he said, ''I guess we ought to follow these buggers and see who they are and what they're up to. How many do you estimate are in the party?''

Gabe dismounted and made a big show of studying the tracks he had already paid close attention to for the past few hours. ''About ten, maybe twelve.''

''Too many for us to mess with,'' Monk said.

But Wyatt Noonan disagreed. ''If they want trouble, we can whip them out on the prairie. With this rifle of mine, I can bring down three or four before they even get into their own rifle range. Long Rider has shown he knows how to handle a Winchester. We could stand off a dozen.''

Purvis Monk wiped his nose on the back of his sleeve. ''A lot of things can go wrong fighting Indians. I was with a couple men about three years ago down near the Canadian River in Texas, and we came across a Comanche hunting party. We thought we had them cold but they started a grass fire and smoked us out into the open. When the smoke cleared, I was riding for my life with four Indians on my tail and the men I was with was all being scalped.''

''The grass here is too green to burn,'' Gabe said, then added a challenge. ''So what are we doing up here if we're not trying to find Indians?''

''All right,'' Noonan snapped. ''We follow them and hope they're friendly so we can make a good powwow. But if they're them damn Blackfeet, I figure we ought to just let them go. The Blackfeet would as soon kill a white man as look at him.''

Monk agreed with that and so did Gabe, who did not think it wise to say that any Indians they found in this part of the country were probably hostiles and would want to shoot first and ask questions later.

They began to travel much faster now that they were after Indians. There was no more talk about railroad grades and where bridges needed to be built over ravines and creeks. Gabe had learned long ago that the best way to travel far and fast on horseback was to put your animal into an easy trot and keep him moving at that gait hour after hour. A good horse could trot four hours at a stretch before its rider needed to stop and let him drink a little water and eat a little grass before starting to trot again. The problem was that few men could withstand the long, grinding punishment of a trotting horse.

Gabe knew he was up to the grueling punishment and did not give a damn if either Purvis Monk or Wyatt Noonan were or not. Let the hard pounding of a trotting horse grind them down physically, until they were jolted out of their socks and their hands shook. It did not concern Gabe.

Hour after hour he led them along the Indian trail, and by evening, Gabe suspected that the warriors they were following were also following someone. He could not be sure, but sometimes there seemed to be two or three additional horses, and the Indians were obviously pushing their mounts to their limits.

By nightfall, both Noonan and Monk had taken all the pounding they could stand, and the big man said, "We camp for the night."

Gabe shook his head. "The Indians are still moving."

"I don't give a damn! This is where we camp. My balls are afire and I ain't riding one more step until tomorrow morning."

"Suit yourself," Gabe said, snatching his Winchester out of its scabbard at the very moment the two men were falling out of their saddles. "But I'm going on alone and I'm afraid that I'll have to trouble you for my six-gun."

Noonan and Monk were professionals and they knew that they had been caught flat-footed and off their guards.

Both men were smart enough not to go for their guns. Given the way they were shaking with fatigue and suffering from six or seven hours of hard pounding, neither man could have drawn and fired very well, anyway.

"He planned this out!" Monk swore. "He made us trot all afternoon just waiting for this moment. I told you we should have killed him."

"Shut up!" Noonan said. "If he'd have planned it out, then why did he want us to keep going?"

"He just said that knowin' we wouldn't."

Gabe chuckled to himself. "If you want to come on, then get back on your horses and lead off. I don't welcome overtaking these Indians all by myself."

Noonan shook his head, then reached his hand down into his pants and massaged his inflamed balls. "I got to rest awhile and so does Purvis. We'll come along at daybreak. You make the peace before we get there."

"*If* we get there," Monk said, his own face drawn with pain as he massaged his crotch and the seat of his pants.

Gabe rode over to Noonan's horse and reached for the hunting rifle and scope. Noonan's hand dipped for his gun but the Winchester in Gabe's hands leveled on his chest and Gabe's warning stopped the man cold. "I won't miss," Gabe promised. "And since I'm the one that's going after the trouble up ahead, I figure this fancy rifle of yours just might come in handy."

"You're leaving me with a six-gun?"

"Monk still has his rifle. It's a hell of a lot better deal than what you'd have left me with the moment you decided I was more trouble than I was worth."

Noonan could not argue that fact. "We'll be coming," he said. "You can just bet your ass we'll be on your backtrail come daylight."

"I'll keep that in mind in case I get into a tight fix," Gabe said, taking the hunting rifle and scope along with his own six-gun, which Noonan had slung over his pommel.

Long Rider backed his horse into the trees and then whirled the animal around on his hind legs and spurred it hard into cover. Noonan and Purvis did not try to shoot at him but that was no comfort to Long Rider. They'd be coming after him in the morning. Purvis Monk wasn't up for the hunt any longer, but Wyatt Noonan . . . Now, he was another breed of cat, and Gabe knew he had shamed the man by getting the drop on him and taking his fancy rifle.

Oh well, a man had to do what a man had to do, and by daybreak, he'd be a good forty miles up the trail and probably sitting down to breakfast with his Indian friends.

When the bright orb of the morning sun poked over the flat tabletop of the eastern plains, Gabe was only a few short miles from the Indians. He had stopped three times during the night so that his sorrel gelding could graze and rest for a half hour while Long Rider catnapped. Gabe knew that the Indians he was chasing were after men, not animals. No buffalo would move fast enough to necessitate this kind of pace.

Gabe rode up a steep bench of land to where he could get a better view, and then he removed the rifle telescope from its case and studied the country to the north until he caught a faint movement. For almost a full minute, he remained perfectly motionless and then lowered the telescope and expelled a deep breath.

"We'll catch them before noon," he said to himself as he spurred the weary sorrel gelding onward.

Long Rider was wrong—he overtook the Indians at midmorning. They were camped by a stream in a thicket of cottonwood trees, and if Gabe had not been very careful, he would have topped a hill and exposed himself to the Blackfeet. But he had guarded himself against that by dismounting before he came to every high place and then peering ahead with caution. Now his foresight had probably saved his life.

Gabe backed on down the hill, out of sight of the war party of Blackfeet. He stood beside his heavily lathered horse for several minutes, just thinking about what he had seen in that brief instant up on the hilltop and what it meant. At last, he came to the inescapable conclusion that the Blackfeet were after a smaller force of their enemies. The enemy might be white men, but more likely they were Sioux or Cheyenne. And it seemed obvious that the smaller band had finally realized they were being hunted and had decided to fight after acknowledging that they could not outdistance their pursuers.

The situation definitely posed a dilemma for Long Rider. If he attempted to reinforce the enemies of the Blackfeet warriors, then he might well be killed in what was sure to be a fight to the death. On the other hand, Gabe did not like Blackfeet any more than he liked the Crow. The Blackfeet had killed many Sioux and had taken many hostages over the centuries. They were traditional enemies and, in addition to that, Gabe was a man who favored taking the side of the underdog.

Decision came to Long Rider quickly. He would trust that the smaller party were either white men, Sioux, or Cheyenne and he would join their numbers. He had, after all, wisely taken the powerful hunting rifle and it could be a great equalizer of unequal forces if used at long range, where its firepower was unequaled.

Gabe's blood quickened as he stepped back into the saddle and rode up into the mountains to circle the Blackfeet encampment. If there were at least five fighting men needing help, then he might be able to make a difference in the outcome. But if there were less, not even the fancy hunting rifle and his own scarred Winchester would make a damn bit of difference against the deadly Blackfeet.

But then, taking the long odds was what made life

interesting and kept a man living on the sharp edge of life. There were no guarantees that you would live to an old age. Hell, even schoolteachers and preachers sometimes died young. Besides, if he were successful in pulling this off, and the men he saved were either Sioux or Cheyenne, then he would be earning their trust.

Long Rider had no fear of death. The only fear he had ever known was the fear of not living his life to the fullest—an experience he had suffered while being locked in an Army prison for nearly three years. To die caged like an animal was unthinkable, to die in battle— now *that* was the only fitting end for a man raised to be a Sioux warrior.

CHAPTER ELEVEN

Long Rider smiled with grim satisfaction when he saw that the four Indians being hunted by the Blackfeet were his cousins, the Hunkpapa, one of the seven "council fires" or tribes of the Sioux. Sitting Bull belonged to the Hunkpapa tribe, while Long Rider, Crazy Horse, and Red Cloud were Oglala. These four Hunkpapa were led by a warrior named Gray Feather, a man that Long Rider knew to be a brave and highly respected fighter.

"Hello, my friends," Gabe called out in the Sioux language as he galloped into their camp wearing the buffalo leather coat that had once been part of his mother's tepee and which carried the faint outline of an Indian thunderbird painted in yellow. "Has the hunter become the hunted?"

The four Hunkpapa recognized their friend at once and Gray Feather said, "Long Rider, you come before a great fight. By this time tomorrow, we will own the scalps of our Blackfeet enemies."

"Strong and good talk," Long Rider said as he dismounted from his horse and held the fancy hunting rifle up for the Hunkpapa to see. Their eyes widened with admiration, and when Long Rider removed the telescopic sight from its leather case and snapped it onto the rifle, they actually laughed and yipped with joy. They knew what the addition of one big hunting rifle in the hands of a man like Long Rider could do and, despite Gray Feather's bold talk, they had prepared to die against so many of the Blackfeet.

"You have a big gun to kill our enemies," Gray Feather said, his eyes never leaving the beautiful rifle. "This will be a day when generations of our children will remember and sing of your greatness."

"It will still be a hard fight," Long Rider said, looking about him and measuring the place where the Hunkpapa had chosen to make what they were sure would be their death stand. Long Rider was pleased for this was a good spot to defend—a rocky knoll with a few trees and a commanding field of fire in every direction. As far as Long Rider could tell, it had only one major fault, and that was that it offered no avenue for retreat nor did it have water.

"How much water do you have?" Long Rider asked.

"Only two small skins," Gray Feather confessed. "We did not expect live long enough to need any more. But now . . ."

"Now we might," Long Rider said. He studied the distant encampment of Blackfeet through the scope. They were all up and watching him and he could see by their gestures that they were very interested in his arrival. Interested, but not the least bit alarmed, and Long Rider knew that they would not have altered their plan of attack because of the addition of a single rider. Instead, it was more likely that the Blackfeet would have celebrated the arrival of one more enemy bringing an additional horse, rifle, and scalp for their lodges.

"Long Rider," Gray Feather said, "you are greatly respected among the native people. I give you the honor of leading us in this fight. You could have ridden past without a sound, but instead, you chose to join us in an honorable way. So you will be our war chief."

Gabe thanked the Indian for such a great honor. He did not immediately say a word but considered every aspect of their situation while the Hunkpapa Indians remained silent out of respect. Gabe had a canteen filled with water but he was still concerned about what might happen if they were pinned on this rocky hillock for several days. But then he remembered Wyatt Noonan and Purvis Monk. At the sounds of distant rifle fire, they were sure to come sneaking up to see the battle and, if the odds were whittled down to about even, Gabe thought they would help.

"You have chosen a good place," he said. "We will rest and wait for the Blackfeet to attack."

Gray Feather was pleased. He was Long Rider's age and if he had been told this place was not suitable, it would have caused him embarrassment. As the minutes passed, they spoke of many things. Of the weather, the hunting, and of people from their tribes that they both knew.

"Where are the buffalo?" Long Rider asked.

"Not far to the north," Gray Feather replied. "We have pushed them into hidden valleys where the white hunters have not yet found them."

"But they will," Long Rider said. "You cannot hide thousands of buffalo."

"There are not so many thousands," Gray Feather said with regret. "Many have been killed for their hides. Many more just for sport. There are some in these mountains that we keep to feed the people during the winter. They are all that keep us free."

"I understand," Long Rider said. "How many Indians are still free?"

"Only three hundred," Gray Eagle said. "But they are good fighters."

Gabe told the Hunkpapa warriors about Aaron Lydick and his railroad plans. As he talked, Gray Feather's expression darkened with anger. "If this man brings his railroad north, we will stop him."

"And I will help you," Long Rider promised. "But bullets and arrows will fail against such a man. We must think of another way to make him stop. This is what I am trying to do now."

"You are wise and also brave," Gray Feather said. "You will think of something. You must make strong medicine."

Long Rider nodded solemnly. "There are two white men with me. I left them behind to come to this fight. But they will be along. You must not tell them what you have told me. They do not speak this language, but they do speak in sign. Tell them nothing about the buffalo or the number of warriors who hunt free and refuse to live on the reservations."

The four Hunkpapa nodded in agreement and Gray Feather said, "What will you tell them?"

"I will tell them the buffalo have all been driven into the Montana country. I will say we will have to go very far to find them. Maybe they will not want to go so far and will turn back."

"This would be good," a warrior named Broken Toe said. "There are buffalo only three days' ride to the north."

Long Rider considered this bit of news. He did not want Purvis Monk and Wyatt Noonan to return to Summer Creek with encouraging news. Better by far that they should report that the buffalo were gone from Wyoming and pushed far, far to the north, maybe even to Canada.

Long Rider heard a high, keening sound and he knew it to be the death chant of the Blackfeet. "They are ready, my brothers. Fight well."

The Blackfeet began to yip and screech, building up their courage, and when they took to their ponies, Long Rider knew that the fight was about to begin. Had he not arrived with the big rifle, the four Hunkpapa would have preferred to have charged down from their little knoll and die attacking the much larger force. But Gabe's sudden and unexpected arrival changed everything. Now, they really believed that they stood a chance of living to tell their village about this great battle. So instead of mounting their ponies and preparing to attack, the Hunkpapa took their places behind the rocks and waited.

It was fortunate that the Hunkpapa warriors had rifles to match those of their enemies. The rifles were mostly single-shot muzzle-loaders instead of the newer rifles that used metallic cartridges. Several of them also had bows and arrows which they would switch to the instant they had fired their rifles knowing that there would be no time to reload before they would be overrun by the Blackfeet.

"Here they come," Long Rider said in a voice loud enough to be heard by his brothers. "I will shoot early and often. Do not let this fool you. Hold your fire until the enemy is very close, and then you must not miss."

Long Rider knew his request would be obeyed by all the Hunkpapa. He looked up at the late-afternoon sun and he said something that would give them all heart. "It is a good day to die for us and also for our enemy. Let us use the next moment well."

By this, Long Rider meant that each of them should reflect upon the Great Spirit who gave them life along with the shining water, the sun, and the earth. And each one of them should thank the Great Spirit for all the days that he had been given and hoped to yet know. But should they die, then the thanks would be remembered by the Great Spirit in the afterworld.

The shrill war cry of the Blackfeet cut the Wyoming prairie's stillness and it was meant to drive fear into the hearts of their enemy. Instead, Long Rider stretched out on the warm earth and laid his cheek against the smooth, polished wood of the hunting rifle. He had never used a telescopic sight before, but he knew it would be easy. There were a set of cross hairs and he laid them dead center on the Blackfoot leader's bead-covered chest. Slowly, with the earth starting to tremble under the hooves of the racing Blackfeet ponies, Gabe squeezed the trigger.

What he saw through the scope was so remarkable that he was momentarily transfixed with wonder. In magnified detail, Long Rider witnessed the effect of the bullet striking his enemy. He saw the Blackfeet's chest explode redly, and the Blackfeet warrior seemed to be lifted up as if jerked by an invisible wire before somersaulting backward over the horse.

The Hunkpapa yipped in glee as Gabe levered another shell into the chamber and again set the cross hairs on a Blackfeet warrior. When he squeezed off the second round, the mounted warrior disappeared.

For an instant, Long Rider felt a deep sense of betrayal as the unfairness of this killing made a strong impact on his mind. The warriors he was shooting had spent their entire lives fighting and training for battle. Their bravery was unquestioned, their skills without peer. It was unjust that they should be killed by a man still a half mile away who was not yet in any personal danger. Shooting men long range was too impersonal. Long Rider could not help shake the feeling that if you took a man's life in a fight, you should at least have to smell him and know that he was a man like yourself instead of a little round picture marked by a set of cross hairs.

Gabe's sense of guilt was so powerful that he actually shoved the rifle away from him for a moment and considered the beautiful and deadly weapon. There was no honor in this for him and when he looked up and saw ten Blackfeet still racing on their painted horses, he understood that it took no courage to set the cross hairs on a man's chest and squeeze the trigger.

He considered this for only a few seconds but during that time, the ten remaining Blackfeet covered a hundred yards, and when the Hunkpapa fired, Gabe was jolted back into reality. The volley unleashed by the Hunkpapa unhorsed two more Blackfeet and a third was hit but managed to stay mounted, his body and those of the other Blackfeet now plastered to the backs of their laboring horses.

Long Rider stood up because he felt compelled to expose himself in plain view as the Blackfeet opened fire. Two of them had repeating Winchester rifles as good as his own, and Gabe saw one of the Hunkpapa grunt and then drop as a bullet struck him in the nose, killing him instantly.

Bullets whip-cracked all around Long Rider as he took aim again through the telescopic sight and fired, knowing even as he pulled the trigger that his target was the same as dead. An instant after he fired, however, a bullet struck the rifle and tore it from his hands. Gabe felt a sharp, deep pain in his left shoulder as he was flung to the earth.

Seeing him down and the big rifle broken, the Blackfeet knew hope, for another Hunkpapa was killed by two bullets that corkscrewed him around in a full circle. The odds were suddenly very much in their favor for now there were only two Hunkpapa and Long Rider who was badly wounded and seemingly helpless against seven mounted Blackfeet.

Gray Feather and the other Hunkpapa warrior dropped their empty rifles and scooped up their bows and arrows. Their aim was true, but the Blackfoot warrior with the repeating rifle shot Gray Feather through the neck, and the Hunkpapa warrior died strangling in his own blood. The last Hunkpapa stood calmly firing arrows and scoring hits until he was knocked off his feet by a bullet. Gabe managed to push himself up on his knees as he yanked his six-gun from his holster and opened fire into the onrushing mass of Indians and horses.

Hundreds of hours of practice had given Gabe the ability to shoot with either hand, and it was a good thing because his left arm hung uselessly at his side as his six-gun bucked repeatedly in his fist, each shot bringing a warrior down.

Gabe ran out of bullets and rolled sideways for his Winchester because it was much faster than the hunting rifle. His first shot brought a death cry from a Blackfoot wearing a red headband, and his second bullet tore a chunk of meat from his enemy's thigh and brought him crashing to the earth, where he tried to rise and attack.

Gabe took aim on the last Blackfoot but before he could pull the trigger, the mounted Indian was knocked screaming from his horse, who vaulted Long Rider and galloped on, its eyes rolling with fear. The last Blackfoot warrior rolled over and over coming to his final rest beside his Sioux enemy.

It was over. The first thing that Long Rider did was reload his six-gun, and the second thing he did was use the butt of his Winchester to push himself to his feet. He hobbled over to the wounded Hunkpapa, a young warrior named Cold Hand, who was hit in the side but appeared to have some chance of surviving if his wound was bound and the bleeding was not internal.

"Are our Blackfeet enemies all dead, Long Rider?" Cold Hand asked in Sioux.

"Yes," he answered. "But our Sioux brothers are also dead."

"Gray Feather and the others will be remembered for their bravery," Cold Hand whispered, looking almost satisfied. "They died well."

Gabe nodded. "But you will not die this day. I'll take you to a white man's doctor and he will make you well."

"No," Cold Hand said, his eyes widening with fear.

"The white doctor will kill me. You must put me on a horse and I will find my own medicine man."

Gabe knew that he had to honor the young Hunkpapa's request. He bound the wound up as well as he could, but the bleeding was very bad and he did not think that Cold Hand would ride far.

Gabe looked up to see Noonan and Monk riding in.

"Is he the only one that's alive besides you?" Noonan asked, jumping off his horse and kneeling beside the young warrior.

"I haven't checked yet, but I think so," Gabe said.

"Purvis will make sure."

Gabe twisted around to see Purvis Monk scalping dead Indians. At that very moment, he was lifting Gray Feather's bloody scalp and the sight filled Gabe with such a rage that he shouted, "Put it down!"

Purvis twisted around with his bloody trophy held up before his eyes. "If you'd a'been killed by these savages, your scalp would be hangin' on one of their lances by now."

"Put it down or I'll kill you," Gabe warned.

Purvis froze and the scalp dropped forgotten to the dirt. "Goddamn you, Indian lover! I've had all I'll take from you!"

"No!" Wyatt Noonan bellowed in vain as Purvis Monk's hand streaked for his gun.

Gabe, wounded and forced to use his right hand with the bent trigger finger, had taken no chances and already started his fast draw. His hand slapped leather and his six-gun leaped up and spat bullets that drilled Purvis Monk through the chest twice before the little gunfighter's own revolver barked harmlessly into the sky.

Purvis staggered backward, tripped over a scalped Indian, and fell hard. Gabe heard the man's lungs empty with force and knew that Purvis Monk was a dead man. He turned his six-gun on Wyatt Noonan and raged, "Are you in the bloody mood for scalping Indians!"

"Hell, no! Don't shoot me, for God's sakes! I came to help you!"

Gabe shook himself like a wet dog and then regained his composure and holstered his six-gun. "Let's get Cold Hand onto his pony."

"He'll be dead before he rides a mile," Noonan said.

"What the hell do you care?"

"If you could save his hide, maybe he could tell Mr. Lydick a thing or two about where the buffalo are hiding."

"They're gone," Long Rider said. "He and the others told me they were all gone."

"I don't believe that for a damn minute," Noonan said in a hard voice. "Where there's Indians, there is buffalo. And in this country we've already found too damn many Indians. I think they've driven the buffalo into hiding someplace and I figure this one can tell us where."

"He's probably going to die," Long Rider said. "You can see that for yourself. I promised he could ride away free and that's what he's going to do."

Noonan was not pleased. "I reckon I'll be telling Mr. Lydick about this when we return to Summer Creek. And I reckon he'll be wonderin' the same as me when it comes to whose side you're on."

"I work for the man that pays me," Long Rider clipped. "But there's no sense in bringing him back a dead man. Come on and help me get him on a horse."

Noonan helped the Hunkpapa warrior to his feet and while Gabe held him up, the big buffalo hunter went to get an Indian pony. He brought it over and they hoisted the badly wounded Indian up into his saddle.

"If you make it," Gabe said, "tell my friends what Long Rider has done and said here."

"I will make it, my brother. And your legend will grow larger than the sun."

Gabe stepped back, his own shoulder wound paining

him mightily. He watched as Cold Hand reined to the north and then rode slowly away.

"Dead within a mile," Noonan growled.

"Don't count on it," Gabe said with pride. "He's Sioux."

CHAPTER TWELVE

Long Rider finished the death scaffolds for the three
Hunkpapa warriors despite Wyatt Noonan's strenuous
protests. It took much of Long Rider's remaining strength
but he would not leave brave Sioux warriors lying on
the prairie for the scavengers to pick their bones clean.

Finally, when it was done, Noonan looked up at the
bodies and growled, "Here we are in Indian country with
maybe a hundred more Blackfeet coming over the next
hill, and you won't leave until this is finished no matter
that you've lost enough blood to full a whiskey keg."

"They would have done the same for me," Gabe said,
feeling weak and dizzy. "I can do no less for them."

"Can you ride?"

"Yes." Gabe struggled over to his sorrel gelding and
tried to lift his foot up into the stirrup but found himself
too weak.

"Shit," Noonan swore. "You're going to die on me
and then I'll be out here by myself. If I run across Indians,

you won't be around to talk us out of getting scalped and I'll be in a hell of a bad fix.''

"Give me a hand up.''

"I'd leave you if we weren't right in the heart of Indian country,'' Noonan groused as he came over and hauled Gabe up into his saddle. "I'd leave you to die the same as you did that young Indian with the hole in his side that just rode north.''

"You have a bad habit of talking too much.''

Now that the burial scaffolding was finished and the work done, Noonan prowled among the Blackfoot dead. "I don't hanker to takin' scalps, but these Indian beads and weapons are always good for a few dollars. Major Pinkerton and that son of a bitch Captain Stone are always ready to buy this stuff to send back east.''

Noonan reached down and pulled a beautiful necklace of turquoise stones and grizzly bear claws from a Blackfoot and held it up to admire. "You don't mind me strippin' these Blackfeet, do you, Long Rider?''

Gabe shook his head and managed to rein his horse south. In his condition, it would take at least six days to reach Summer Creek—if he could make it at all. And he'd never make it if he didn't start moving right now.

"I'll catch up with you before dark!'' Noonan shouted as he worked over the bodies.

Gabe did not even look back. He leaned over his saddle horn and concentrated on staying upright. The only good thing he could think about that had happened out here was that he had learned a few things from Gray Feather about the buffalo and the number of Indians who had taken refuge outside the reservations. Other than that, the trip had proven to be a near disaster. Purvis was dead and Gabe suspected that Lydick would not be one bit pleased when he learned that he'd been shot by Long Rider.

Gabe twisted around in his saddle and the effort cost him a grunt of pain. He could still see Noonan searching

the bodies and maybe even scalping them for all that
Gabe knew. Wyatt Noonan was a strange man. He didn't
exactly fit any particular mold or do what was expected.
That made him even more dangerous than some reckless
hothead like Purvis Monk, whose actions and reactions
had been entirely predictable.

Gabe turned back around in his saddle and kept riding.
His shoulder hurt like blazes and so did his back. Still,
he knew he was lucky just to be alive and that he'd stay
alive to see this trouble through.

To push away the pain, Gabe decided to think of something that felt good. Without a moment's hesitation, he
remembered Annie Rooney and Holly Brown. Holly with
her pretty smile and soft lips, Annie Rooney with her
lush breasts and insatiable female passion. Just thinking
about making love to Annie caused Long Rider's manhood to stiffen, and that brought a grin despite his
wounds.

Yeah, he thought, Annie would know how to make
me feel a hell of a lot better if she were here right now.

Annie Rooney was down, but not for the count. Not
quite, at least. The powerful young blacksmith had her
new riding habit pulled up to her waist and was trying
to pry her legs open while at the same time unbuttoning
the front of his trousers.

"Damn you, John Horner!" she screamed, far more
angry than frightened. "You promised me before we left
Summer Creek that you'd be a gentleman if I let you
come along to find Long Rider! You said nothing would
happen between us!"

"I lied," he panted. There was also pleading in his
voice. "Annie, I already asked you ten times already to
marry me. And the last time, you said yes. So there's
no damn reason we need to wait to consummate our
love!"

He finally managed to tear his thick rod out of his

trousers. "Come on, Annie, we're in love!"

"You put that big, ugly thing back in your pants or, so help me, I'll twist it off you!" Annie cried, grabbing his already-stiff rod with both hands and giving it a hard twist that brought the man straight up on his knees. "Put it back, I say!"

Before he could even yelp, big John Horner felt her reach into his pants, grab his testicles, and mash them together tightly. He threw himself back with a scream and scrambled away from her. Groaning in pain, he shouted in anger, "I swear I don't know why you're doin' this to me! I love you and you're driving me crazy for wanting to prove it."

"You don't have to 'prove it.' I know you love me and I want to make sure it stays that way."

"Huh?"

"You heard me," Annie said, pulling her riding habit down over her knees and pinning it to her ankles. "Every time I've let a man have his pleasure with me, he's immediately lost interest."

"I'll never lose interest."

"Damn right, you won't," Annie said, climbing to her knees and wiping the grass off the back of her dress. "You are going to marry me but not until I have a chance to explain to Long Rider why I'm not sticking with him."

"Dammit!" Horner exploded. "Long Rider don't love you! Everyone in town saw him sparkin' Holly Brown."

"He does too love me!" Annie snapped. "And I loved him for a time. We declared our love, John. Now I can't let him come back to Summer Creek and find us married. It wouldn't be right."

"He might be dead out here and if we don't be careful, *we'll* be dead, too. This is Indian country. And if they don't get us, Aaron will when he finds out what I've been up to out here."

Annie made an unladylike gesture to emphasize her point. "Screw Aaron Lydick! I'm sick to death of hearing his name. I wish you'd be man enough to stop worrying whether or not he approves of every damn thing you do.''

Stung deeply, Horner popped to his feet and advanced threateningly. ''Oh yeah! Well, if I was afraid of Mr. Lydick, I sure wouldn't be out here riskin' my neck for you, now would I?''

''No,'' Annie said, the anger washing out of her. ''I guess you wouldn't at that. I really do love you, John. But I got to find Long Rider and tell him the way of it before we can get married.''

The blacksmith shoved his now-flaccid manhood back into his pants and angrily buttoned them back up. ''You're about the stubbornest woman I ever did see. But I don't understand how we're supposed to find Long Rider out here all alone ourselves. This is damn big country. We lost his tracks and the best thing we could do is to wait until he shows up again.''

''I can't do that,'' Annie said. ''He may be in trouble.''

''*We* may be in trouble.''

''If you're too afraid to ride on, then go back and . . . and bend some damn horseshoes!''

''I'm going with you if we have to go all the way to Canada. But if Indians jump us and it looks like the end, you got to promise me one thing.''

Curious, Annie raised her eyebrows. ''And just what would that be?''

''I'd want to die a satisfied man,'' he said earnestly.

Her eyebrows shot up even farther and she had to struggle to keep from giggling. ''You mean . . . you mean you'd want to do it together with Indians about to lift our hair?''

''I sure as hell would,'' Horner said, feeling embarrassed but still determined to reach some sort of an understanding. ''I'd just like to think that I got something out of all this trouble before I was scalped.''

Annie placed her hands on her shapely hips and laughed outright. "John, I do declare! That's about the most flattering thing any man ever said to me. Of course I'd let you have your way with me if I thought we were going to get killed by Indians."

"All right, then," he said, feeling he'd finally eked out a little victory. "Then let's ride on."

Two days later, they met Long Rider and Wyatt Noonan. Long Rider was unconscious and lying on a travois that the big buffalo hunter had fashioned.

"He's got a bullet in his shoulder that's festerin'," Noonan explained with a shrug of his wide shoulders to indicate that he did not give a damn. "I figured that I had to at least try and get him to a doctor."

Annie threw herself from her saddle and rushed to Long Rider's side. She pulled his blood-crusted shirt aside and looked at the purple blotches that were spreading like angry fingers in all directions outward from the terrible shoulder wound. She also touched his forehead and felt the raging temperature.

"He'll be dead before we can get him to Summer Creek," she said, looking up at both men. "We're going to have to dig the bullet out."

"Not me," Noonan said. "I tried that once and killed a friend. I won't do any better on a man I have sworn to kill."

"I'll help you," Horner said.

Annie slipped her fingers back behind the shoulder in the desperate hope that she might feel the bullet. Realizing the futility of that, she looked around them and said, "There's a grove of aspen over there by that stream. We had better get him over there out of the sun before we open up that wound."

"Whoever you are, mister, you drag him over there and then you ride hard for Summer Creek and tell the doctor that he's needed."

"The doc's name is Milburn and he sure as hell won't

ride three days into Indian country risking his neck for a stranger.''

''How far west are we from Mr. Lydick's railroad?''

Noonan frowned. ''Hell, I guess we aren't more than thirty or forty miles.''

Annie had figured about the same. ''Then I suggest you tell Mr. Lydick about this and have him bring the doctor up on his railroad, then ride over here as fast as he can.''

''I'll tell him,'' Noonan said, his hand on the hunting rifle that was back in its scabbard alongside Gabe's Winchester. He had also taken the man's six-gun and shoved it into his saddlebags. Hell, Long Rider was going to die, so he damn sure wouldn't need either weapon again.

Noonan frowned. ''But if Long Rider dies before we get back, I don't think we're gonna shed any tears. You see, he's a damn injun lover.''

''Just git over to them trees!'' Annie yelled at the man.

Noonan spurred his horse over to the side of the stream and then hopped down and cut the bindings, ridding himself of the travois. The travois dropped down heavily to the earth, causing Long Rider to moan and thrash.

''Damn you!'' Annie raged. ''Get out of here!''

''Happy to do that,'' Noonan said, eyeing the saucy young woman and the powerful blacksmith.

He absently scratched his crotch for a moment, thinking how easy it would be to draw his gun and shoot the blacksmith and Long Rider. He could spend a few exciting and pleasurable hours with the woman and then leave her, take all the horses, and ride on.

He was in serious need of a woman but the whole thing seemed too complicated so he decided it would just be easier to ride over to Fort York instead. He'd sell the Blackfoot and Sioux necklaces which he'd climbed up to strip, then maybe spend a couple of days with some squaw who had a husband low-down enough to sell her for the price of a jug of whiskey. Afterward, with plenty of ready cash still in his pockets, he'd take his time and ride over to Summer Creek. With any luck at all, Long Rider would be dead and there wouldn't be much to tell Mr. Lydick, anyway.

"He sure ain't riding off in any hurry," John said.

Annie shook her head. "He's hopin' that Long Rider dies, and I wouldn't be surprised if he'd like to see us get scalped."

"Then it's up to us."

Annie rolled up her sleeves. "That's right. Fortunately, I've done a little mending of men in my time."

She took Long Rider's knife and tested its cutting edge. It was sharp enough to draw a thin line of blood on the tip of her thumb, which she sucked clean. "If you'll gather some firewood and start a fire, we'll get this over with as soon as we can."

The blacksmith looked thoughtfully down upon Long Rider for a long moment before he asked, "You ain't going to fall back in love with him if he lives, are you?"

"Nope." Annie carefully pulled off Gabe's shirt. "But does it matter right now?"

"No, I guess not." Horner left to gather the wood while Annie went to their horse and found the beat-up old coffeepot they'd brought along. She washed it out in the creek, listening to her blacksmith tear dead limbs from trees and thinking how strong and admirable he was. A little too impatient and pretty randy, but that was good because she required a lot of man to satisfy her own needs.

Annie washed the coffeepot again and filled it with creek water. Ten minutes later, they had a fire and the pot was beginning to simmer as smoke drifted up through the tree branches.

"You're going to have to hold him down tight. When I cut into his shoulder and start diggin' for the bullet, he's gonna buck and hump like a lassoed mustang."

The blacksmith eyed her with new respect. "It takes a lot of courage to dig into someone."

"Courage hasn't a thing to do with it," Annie said, passing the blade of the knife through the fire and then dipping it into the boiling water. "It's do it or else watch a good man die."

She took a deep breath and plunged the tip of Gabe's knife straight down into the wound. Pus and putrid corruption spurted out around the knife blade, and Annie damn near vomited at the smell. Instead, she gritted her teeth and kept working the blade, even as Long Rider cried out and began to thrash under the weight of the blacksmith.

"It's the worst I ever saw," Annie said in a small voice. "Might be gangrene. I don't know if there's any hope at all."

She felt beads of sweat pop out across her forehead and they ran down to sting her eyes as she concentrated on cutting and the feeling for the lead ball deep inside Gabe's shoulder. She sliced the bad flesh loose and pulled it out with her fingers, hurling it away from her sight. When the wound finally began to ooze with red blood, she knew that she was at least getting the corrupted flesh cleaned out so that the shoulder had a chance of healing properly.

Pushing two fingers into the hole, she closed her eyes and tried to feel the hard bullet. Failing that, she swallowed her disappointment, opened her eyes, and said, "Roll him over."

"What!"

"The bullet is too deep to get out from the front. I got to try and get it out from the back."

"He'll die on us for sure."

"He'll die for sure if I don't get it out! Now, please, John, roll him over and climb astraddle his back."

Gabe had stopped thrashing and when he was rolled over, the blacksmith climbed onto his back and gripped both shoulders. "Jesus Christ," he whispered, staring at the second bullet wound that had ripped angrily across Gabe's back. "I don't know what's kept the man alive!"

Annie took a deep breath. She wanted a drink and she wanted to run, but instead she placed the tip of the blade against the flesh and prayed that she had it figured the location about right. Jamming the blade deep into the unmarked flesh was the hardest thing she had ever done, and Gabe actually screamed and almost succeeded in throwing the blacksmith off, even though he was still unconscious.

"Hold him steady!"

"I'm trying!"

Annie twisted the blade and thought she felt it's edge touch something hard. It might be a bone, but it might also be a bullet. "Just hang on," she whispered, cutting deeper and then slipping a forefinger in alongside of the wet blade until she felt the bullet. "I found it!"

"Get the damned thing out!"

"I'm trying!"

Annie again closed her eyes and this time her fingernail slipped over the bullet and pinned it to the slippery blade. An instant later, she popped the lead ball out and almost collapsed on Long Rider.

"Get some green leaves and bark for a poultice," she said in a voice weak with fatigue. "I have to let him bleed for a few more minutes to get all the poison out."

"I didn't know a man had so much blood inside of him," Horner said, falling off Gabe and looking drained.

Annie gave a silent, heartfelt prayer that her effort had not been in vain. She felt for Gabe's pulse and it was almost nonexistent. She was afraid that he would die despite her crude attempt at at surgery, but at least he now had a slim chance of survival. Had she not removed the bullet, he'd certainly have been dead within another twenty-four hours. Either way, she would not regret having tried to save this man.

"Here you go," Horner said, shoving some leaves and bark at her.

Annie crumpled the leaves up and dropped them into the coffeepot, which had already begun to simmer. She added the bark and let it boil for several minutes. "I'll need your shirt for a bandage," she said. "I'll have to bind the poultice to him both front and back."

Horner quickly removed his shirt. "You were wonderful," he said, unable to keep his eyes off her.

Annie blushed and then stirred the bark and leaves, saying, "I did what I had to do, and you'll know how to do the same for me if I ever get shot."

His admiring smile died at the thought of her being shot.

"Here," Annie said, pulling the coffeepot out of the fire, "help me get this stuff out of the coffeepot and onto the wound."

"It'll scald his flesh, it's so hot."

"After what he's just been through," Annie said, "he won't mind so very much."

Two days later, Long Rider was still alive and the purple fingers of death that had been reaching for his laboring heart were shriveling and fading away.

"I think he's going to live," Annie whispered, unable to contain the excitement she felt inside.

Horner glanced past the woman and his eyes widened with momentary fear, which he quickly hid. "Annie," he said, in a voice grown old. "I have to tell you something."

She looked up suddenly, aware that his face had grown suddenly old. "What's wrong?"

"Take a look to the north."

Annie twisted around and saw the Indians. They were a good three miles out but they were coming fast and lined up abreast. She counted no less than twenty.

"We can get to the horses and run for it," Horner said without enthusiasm.

"And how far would we get before they overtook us and drove spears into our backs? Five miles? Ten miles? No more." Annie shook her head. "No, we stay here and fight to the death."

He nodded. "I knew that would be your answer."

"And you agree?"

He reached for her hand and his voice was urgent. "I want you to run for it while I stay here and hold them back. I'm not a good shot, but they won't know that. Maybe . . ."

Annie touched his lips. "Uh-uh. I'm not going anywhere without you. Not ever again."

Tears filled his eyes and he roughly brushed them aside. Annie forced a smile and then pulled her dress up around her waist and whispered, "Love me while there is still time for us."

John Horner did not have to be asked twice. He tore open the front of his trousers and, to his amazement, he discovered that he was already hard. Forcing the advancing Indians out of his mind, he gathered Annie into his powerful arms, and when her hips lifted, he drove his thick root up inside of her.

Annie moaned with pleasure. She held him tightly, feeling him deep inside of her, and then she locked her thighs around his powerful buttocks and said, "We have about three, maybe four minutes before they are in rifle range. Can we do it that fast?"

He growled with pleasure and began to thrust himself into her with a frenzy born of desperation. Annie was caught up in his passion and all too soon, they were both thrashing and straining, gasping and lunging until they stiffened and Annie cried out with pleasure, not caring that the warriors were surely watching her now.

Horner's buttocks stiffened and he groaned as his body

jerked, quickly emptying his seed into the woman he loved.

For a moment, they clung to each other, neither wishing to break back to the reality of their impending death. But Annie finally said, "Let's give them a fight."

Horner nodded, then twisted around to the north. They both saw the Indians and, to their utter amazement, the entire line of mounted warriors had halted to watch their energetic coupling.

"Holy cow!" Horner breathed. "What's the matter with them? Haven't they ever seen a white woman and a white man couple? Did they think we did it different, or what!"

He sounded angry.

Annie rolled him off her and pulled down her skirt as she grabbed up a rifle. She remembered how Long Rider had expertly made love to her and she knew he had learned to satisfy a woman while living among the Indians. Annie said, "They do it the same as us. Maybe they like to watch."

Horner tore the rifle from her and was furious. "Well, I'll give them something to watch!" he stormed as he raised the rifle and started to fire.

"Wait!" Annie cried, knocking the rifle down. "Look!"

Horner dropped the rifle a fraction of an inch. "Holy cow," he breathed. "The one in the headdress has his hand up in the sign of peace!"

Annie could not help herself. She began to laugh hysterically because of a flooding sense of relief as well as the astonishing picture she and John must have just presented to the Indians.

"What the hell is so funny!" he demanded hotly.

When she could stop laughing, Annie flung herself into John's arms and cried, "Don't you get it?—They're *Sioux* Indians. They've come to help Long Rider!"

The blacksmith's jaw dropped and his eyes widened with surprise. Then, with his forgotten root still hanging out of his pants, he buried his face in Annie's hair and sighed with relief.

CHAPTER THIRTEEN

The leader of the Sioux was a chief named Black Elk, a tall, dignified warrior who had led over a hundred of the Hunkpapa Sioux off the reservation and had taken them into the Big Horn Mountains three years earlier. And even though the United States Army under Major Pinkerton had spent years trying to trap and force Black Elk into submitting to reservation life, the chief had always managed to elude the soldiers.

Now, Black Elk tried to keep his face composed as he watched the white man and white woman wildly coupling on the prairie grass. He did not dare look either to the left or right for he was afraid his great amusement would be seen by his men and that they would begin to laugh.

When the coupling was done, Black Elk was impressed mostly by the young woman, but also by the man. He raised his hand and when the white man grabbed up his rifle, Black Elk did not lower his hand to prove his own bravery. Besides, he reasoned, what man could shoot straight with his tool dangling ridiculously out of his pants?

A moment later, when the white man lowered his gun and Black Elk heard laughter, he was confused and lowered his hand. Frowning with disapproval, he kicked his buckskin pony forward and the line of warriors on either side of him followed.

Black Elk was conversant in the white man's language, though he thought English to be overly complicated and wordy. Still, he alone among his people could speak English well, and this was a thing that brought him a great measure of pride as well as respect.

"I am Black Elk of the Hunkpapa," he called as he rode nearer. "I come in peace to take Long Rider to our medicine man."

Annie and John both held up their hands and Annie said, "I am Annie Rooney and this is John Horner. You speak good English, chief of the Hunkpapa. Long Rider is also our friend. I am good medicine for him."

"You are good medicine for any man," Black Elk said with admiration for her energetic coupling skill. With a twinkle of mirth in his dark eyes, he slipped from his buckskin and walked over to kneel beside Long Rider. He pulled Gabe's shirt aside and was surprisingly gentle when he removed the fresh poultices from the shoulder wound. He studied the large, ugly hole for several minutes, then eased Gabe over onto his side and examined the exit incision that Annie had made to remove the bullet.

"You do this, little woman?"

"Yes, with my man's help."

"You do good job," Black Elk said. He eased Long Rider back down and touched his face. He motioned for a man who wore a yellow zigzag of paint on each of his cheeks and a red hawk painted on his forehead to come down from his horse. The man hurried forward, a rattle in his fist. He was old, with gray hair, bad teeth, and a quick, almost birdlike nervousness. Without preliminaries, he knelt beside Gabe and pried open his mouth.

"Hey!" Annie protested when the man opened a small leather pouch and retrieved a pinch of herbs and seeds, "What is he doing?"

"He make good medicine," Black Elk said. "You wait and see."

Annie started to say something but Horner silenced her with a hard squeeze of his hand. The old Sioux sprinkled his medicine into Gabe's mouth, then took a small skin of water mixed with something, pulled a tiny horn-tip stopper loose, then poured brackish-looking water into Gabe's open mouth before he pushed the jaw up and held it closed. This accomplished, he threw his head back and began to make a strange, almost growling sound deep in his throat that was punctuated every few seconds by a sharp yipping that made him sound very much like a coyote.

"What is he doing?" John asked with bewilderment.

"He is praying to the Great Spirit that the medicine he has just given Long Rider will soon bring him strength and wakefulness."

Black Elk turned to his warriors and spoke to them rapidly in their own tongue. Four of them went into the aspen forest and began to cut slender poles.

"Your travois no good," Black Elk said, making a face that clearly indicated he thought the job that Wyatt Noonan had done was very poor.

Annie was outraged. "You can't move him now! His wounds are just beginning to heal."

"Like Cold Hand, he live," Black Elk said, speaking to John Horner, for it was considered beneath his dignity to argue with a woman, even one that was white and coupled so energetically. "We go before white men come back."

To indicate his concern, he pointed to the tracks that

Noonan had made heading south, which three of his warriors had been ordered to follow in order to give the chief fair warning of any unwelcome visitors.

"But a white doctor is coming!" Annie protested. "We've sent for help. Go away."

Black Elk was resolute in his own determination. "Long Rider one of the People. He come with us. You can come, too."

"All right, we will!"

"Now, wait a minute!" John exclaimed. "Why do we need to go with them? You know Long Rider is going to be in good hands."

"I know nothing of the sort and I still haven't been able to tell him about us, so I have to go."

"Holy cow!" John swore in exasperation. "Do you know what you're saying! You're saying that you want us to go with these people to God only knows where for a reason I can't even begin to imagine!"

"Trust me," Annie said. "They aren't going to hurt us. They offered us the sign of peace and Black Elk even speaks English. Look at this as an adventure. Once I explain to Long Rider about us, we can ride back to Summer Creek."

"This is insane!"

Annie smiled sweetly and looked at Black Elk. "We will come to your village. Is it far?"

Black Elk simply nodded his head and turned away, to stand facing the south. "You will tell me about the new iron horse that comes into our lands," he said in a cold voice.

Annie's smile died on her lips. "Yes, I will tell you about the iron horse, and so will Long Rider. I believe that is why he is here now. To stop the iron horse and to save your buffalo."

At the word *buffalo* Black Elk swung around and his eyes bored into her so hotly that Annie took an involuntary step backward. "What's wrong?"

The chief did not reply but was fairly shaking with anger, and John Horner stepped in front of Annie and whispered nervously, "Please don't say the word *buffalo* again!"

"Yeah," Annie said, "I think you're right."

The Indians ate pemmican, which Annie learned was a dried lean meat mixed with fat and pounded into flat cakes. The pemmican was as tough as rawhide but good, and both Annie and John discovered they were famished.

Within an hour, the travois was readied, and Long Rider was gently placed on its leather bindings, then tied firmly in position. Black Elk made the sign that it was time to leave, and almost as if by magic, the three scouts who had ridden south appeared on the horizon to swiftly rejoin them.

Annie watched Long Rider's drawn face and then reached out and touched John Horner. "I'm glad we did it together even if I will lose you like all the others."

"Lose me, hell! I can hardly wait until tonight when we camp so that you and I can do it all over again, only this time in private."

Annie giggled girlishly and her excitement was so high she blurted, "What a wonderful adventure this is!"

The blacksmith looked at her eyes shining with life and even he had to admit it was so. Maybe he was going to lose his stable and shop when Aaron Lydick learned what he'd done, but right now, he figured it was worth it. Besides, now that he'd been away from Summer Creek for a few days, he'd taken on a whole new perspective about things. Maybe Summer Creek was too small and too rigid in its obedience to Aaron Lydick, and maybe he and Annie would be better off to just say screw it, and move on.

Aaron Lydick stood behind his desk and said in a voice that shook with anger, "What the hell do you mean, 'Long Rider shot Purvis Monk to death and then ran off to help some Indians stand off more Indians'?''

Wyatt explained it all over again, this time leaving out nothing except the fact that he had stripped the Indian bodies of their necklaces and other adornments and then rode to Fort York and sold them to the Army officers. What a time he'd had! His head still ached from all the whiskey he'd drunk, and he'd lost himself for three days with a pair of Crow squaws that had damn near succeeded in screwing him to death. No, it would not do to tell Aaron that he had dallied and debauched himself thoroughly before riding over to Summer Creek with his news.

Wyatt was not physically afraid of Aaron Lydick, though he knew the man was entirely capable of hiring some other gunman to challenge him to a draw. What Wyatt was concerned about was money, because Aaron paid very well.

''So it's like I said, boss. I had to leave Long Rider, the girl, and that damn blacksmith because they refused to come back here and explain things. I don't know what happened to them. All I know for sure is that Long Rider was pretty badly shot up and I don't expect he lived.''

''And you found no buffalo!''

''Well, boss, you can't hardly blame that on me, now can you?''

''How far north did you and Purvis take Long Rider?''

''Three hundred miles at least.'' It was a bald-faced lie but he said it without batting an eyelash. ''We traveled nearly two weeks.''

''Three hundred miles and not a single buffalo! How am I supposed to fulfill my contracts? How am I going to make a profit on my damned railroad? Everyone I've ever talked to said I'd find buffalo less than two hundred miles north of the Union Pacific line! And you're telling me there's none within three hundred? I don't believe it!''

Wyatt Noonan had never allowed any man to call him

a liar and he didn't intend to allow it to happen now. But Lydick hadn't actually come out and said he was a liar, so Wyatt gave him the benefit of the doubt and held his tongue.

Lydick began to pace back and forth and, as was his habit, he talked his thoughts out loud. "I'll bet those goddamn hostile Indians up north have rounded up the buffalo and driven them into the Big Horns or some other mountains where they'll be hard to find. But the herds are up there, make no mistake about that. By God, they are up there and I mean to find and slaughter them all!"

Lydick wheeled around and stabbed a finger in Wyatt's direction. "You say that Long Rider was shot?"

"That's right."

"Where? Point it out to me exactly."

Wyatt touched an index finger about halfway between the end of his shoulder and his left nipple. "About there."

"Impossible," Aaron snapped with impatience. "He'd have taken the bullet through the lung and died within the hour. You know that."

Wyatt colored. "All right, damnit!" he swore, moving his finger toward the end of his shoulder to indicate a less serious wound. "Here, then. I do know that he wasn't lung shot. There was no blood on his lips and no bloody bubbles. I couldn't hear any suckin' sounds so I know it missed his lungs."

"Then there is a real possibility that he's still alive." Lydick took a cigar out of a silver box, not bothering to offer one to Wyatt. "And if he's alive, he will be with the Sioux by now and he'll be warning them of my plans. Wouldn't you agree?"

Wyatt realized the railroad man's logic was sound. Long Rider had proven his real loyalty to the Indian when he'd gone to help the four Sioux Indians under attack by the Blackfeet. "Yes sir, I agree."

"Then if they have been warned, there is no chance

whatsoever that they will cooperate, and that means I must use force to exert my will and drive my railroad north to where I can find their damn herds and meet my orders from the Army and the East.''

"Then you're sayin' you want to take a big force of men north and attack the Indians?" Wyatt shook his head. "Even with all your money it'll be hard finding gunmen willing to go up there into Indian territory. That's Custer country.''

Lydick lit his cigar, blew a smoke ring, and jammed his finger through it toward his hired gun. "You don't understand," the railroad man said. "I won't have to hire anyone but you . . . and Captain William Stone, who will lead a battalion of cavalry up north to the Powder River country, where we will root out the hostiles and force them to reveal where they have hidden their damn buffalo.''

"He'll do that?"

"Sure, he will.''

Wyatt shook his head. "That's a lot of responsibility for a captain. What will Major Pinkerton say?''

"Major Pinkerton will receive an urgent telegraph from Washington asking him to come back to the East at once. And in his absence, Captain Stone will again become the acting commander of Fort York. He understands how important fresh buffalo meat will become for his soldiers this winter. I am just sure of it.''

Wyatt had to click his tongue in admiration. "Who else but you could get the United States Army to do his dirty work? Boss, you got everything figured out down to crossin' the T's and dottin' the I's, don't you.''

"Damn right, I do. But occasionally even I make a grievous mistake. The worst I've made throughout this whole damn thing is thinking that I could buy Long Rider with money and the promise to help his people—which I would not have done. Still, I was convinced that every man has his price. But Long Rider proved me wrong.''

Lydick walked around behind his desk and pulled out a sheet of writing paper from his top left-hand drawer. He inked a quill and began to write a letter. "You will take this to the telegraph office at Rawlins and send it at once. Make sure that it is seen only by the operator named Blevins. He's a man who has proven his worth to me many times and can keep his mouth shut. Give it to Mr. Blevins and then ride on back to Fort York."

"To watch Major Pinkerton go racin' off to Washington?"

"Exactly. And when he is gone, you may give the second letter I am about to write to Captain Stone, who will begin to prepare for his military campaign with great alacrity."

Lydick finished the telegram and took another sheet of paper out of his desk and began to dictate to himself. "Dear Captain Stone. It has come to my attention that three white people have been attacked, perhaps killed and certainly wounded and possibly abducted by hostile Indians up near the Powder River. Please act with great haste and meet me and Mr. Wyatt Noonan along with a battalion of your men at the northern vanguard of my railroad. We must save these people!"

Noonan chuckled. "I take it you're not going to tell him that one of the white people is Long Rider, the Indian lover?"

"Hell, no. Now, what would I gain by doing a foolish thing like that?"

"Beats the devil out of me," Noonan said, taking both letters, folding them up, putting them inside his coat pocket, and heading for the door.

"Wyatt?"

He stopped and turned around. "Yeah?"

Lydick's eyes shuttered and his voice took on an edge. "The next time you have important news for me, you'd damn sure better not be selling Indian necklaces and jewelry to the officers at Fort York and whoring away your money on disease-ridden squaws while I cool my heels. Do you understand me clearly?''

Wyatt Noonan was a brave man, but there was something in the warning that caused an involuntary shiver to ripple up and down his spine. He did not have to ask who had spied on him during his orgy of sex and drinking while spending his money at Fort York. Hell, maybe Captain Stone himself had passed the word back to Summer Creek.

''Do you understand me!'' Aaron roared.

''Yes, sir!''

Lydick blew smoke at his face. ''Good. Now get the hell over to Rawlins and have my man send that telegram, and then get your ass over to Fort York and wait for further instructions. And you'd better stay off the squaws and keep sober.''

Thoroughly shamed, Wyatt Noonan shoved through the door and out into the street. He trembled with pent-up humiliation and shame but went straight for his horse, and as Aaron Lydick watched him through the window, the railroad man knew that he would not mess up again.

CHAPTER FOURTEEN

Long Rider stared up at Annie's pretty face, ringed by the sun that lanced down through his tepee's smoke hole. He only half listened as Annie struggled to explain how she had fallen in love with her handsome young blacksmith, John Horner, and intended to marry him.

"I feel awful after how I swore I'd love you forever," she said lamely. "But I knew right from the start that you weren't a marrying man. Not like John. He wants to marry me and I do love him, though not as fiercely as I loved you. He smells like a horse and he isn't the poet you are, but he's honest and handsome and he will be true to me. I know that. I'm sorry if I've hurt you, but I have to do this."

Long Rider tried to look hurt and resigned to this terrible news. "I shouldn't be too crushed because I knew from the first moment I saw him that John Horner was in love with you, Annie. And to be honest, I even suppose I should admit that you've made the right choice.''

"I have?" Annie didn't look as if she was too pleased by this admission. "Well, I was . . ."

"It's true," Gabe said, touching her cheek and trying not to think about how good it would be to make love to her again, even in his debilitated condition.

"Really?" Annie frowned. "You must be terribly disappointed."

"Yeah," Long Rider fibbed. "I am, but you saved my life and I know he'll make you a better husband than I would have."

"Well, that's what I thought, too," she said, looking down into his gray eyes and still wondering if she'd made a big mistake. "I mean, you're a white man but it's easy to see by the way these people treat you that you're a respected leader among the Sioux. For all I know, you might have even decided to take up living permanently with these people and I'd never have been happy in a tepee."

"You're not comfortable?"

"Oh sure! Chief Black Elk married us the Indian way, which was real nice. Wasn't much to it, but I sort of wanted it formal-like and he laughed and went along with my silliness."

"It wasn't silliness," Gabe said, correcting her. "An Indian wedding might not have much pomp and ceremony to it but it's just as binding as a white man's wedding. And I understand that you've got your own buffalo-hide tepee and everything."

"We sure do!" Annie chuckled. "I'm for staying through the fall and then going back to Summer Creek and settling our business and moving on to California."

"What about your husband?"

"He says he wants to decide when he gets back. John sort of likes Summer Creek. And if it wasn't for Aaron

Lydick ownin' and runnin' everyone there, it wouldn't be such a bad place to live.''

"It would be a good place to live," Gabe said. "But I've got to tell you that I intend to stop that northern railroad any way that I can.''

"I know that. John and I have talked it over and we'd like to help.''

"Uh-uh," Gabe said, pushing himself up into a sitting position. "This fight is between the Indian and that railroad.''

"And the United States Army," Annie said. "You and these people don't stand a chance of winning. Best thing you can do is to try and make the best deal you can with Aaron.''

"You're probably right," Gabe admitted. "Help me up, will you? Black Elk has called a council fire and we're going to talk about what we can do.''

Annie helped Gabe to his feet. He was barechested and the shoulder wounds were scabbed over but healing cleaningly as was the bullet wound across his back. On impulse, Annie lightly touched the wound, remembering how she had dug into his flesh with his own knife and removed the corruption.

She shuddered at the memory and said, "You're sure scarred up but you're still a hell of a fine-looking man.''

"Better not let your new husband hear you say that or we'll both be in deep trouble," Gabe warned. "Help me get on a shirt and point me toward Black Elk's tepee.''

Annie did as he asked. "Will you come and tell me and John what you decide?''

"All right.''

"That's a promise?''

"You've my word on it," Gabe grunted as he bent over and pulled on his boots, then tucked his shirt into his pants, and headed stiffly out of the tepee.

"His tepee is that huge one in the center of the village," Annie said, pointing it out to him.

"Of course," Long Rider said. "The one with the Black Elk painted on it. What else?"

"We'll be waiting for you."

"I want to wash in the stream and take a sweat bath before I come to visit," he said. "My body is unclean and I need time to be alone with my thoughts."

Annie nodded. "That's our tepee over there. The one with the yellow sun painted on it. Kind of pretty, I think. Anyway, we'll be waiting."

Gabe looked at the tepee and saw the squat, powerful John Horner sitting in front of it on a buffalo robe. He looked worried. "Tell your man I offered you my congratulations."

"Tell him yourself when you come to visit and eat with us," Annie said.

"I will," Gabe promised, heading for Black Elk's tepee.

This was his first look at the Hunkpapa village and he was surprised at its size. There were at least forty tepees scattered across a wide, grassy meadow. Each tepee was painted with the symbols of its owner. As Long Rider moved alone through the village, he became aware that women and children stopped their work and play to stare at him.

A boy of about five approached shyly and presented him with a fine bird's nest, and Long Rider knelt and pretended to inspect it with great interest. Speaking in Sioux, he said to the child, "This is the nest of the meadowlark, one of the most intelligent of all the birds and one who is very watchful of all dangers. Just as the People must always be watchful of dangers. Thank you for this fine present. I will keep it to remind me that life is full of dangers and we must be vigilant at all times."

He stood up and, cradling the small bird's nest as if it were a great prize, walked with dignity through the camp until he came to the extra-large tepee of Black Elk.

He was greeted by the chief, who said, "Welcome,

Long Rider. Come inside with me to talk with the people of the things that we must do to stop the iron horse and the soldiers who come.''

Long Rider had just begun to step inside the tepee when he froze. "How do you know that soldiers come?"

"We have eyes that can see farther than the rifle glasses that you have used," Black Elk explained. "They come in great numbers. Many horse soldiers."

Long Rider pushed inside the tepee and the first warrior he saw was Cold Hand. "Greetings, my brother!" the Hunkpapa said, starting to rise to his feet.

"Stay seated," Long Rider said, greeting the other Indian leaders who had gathered to discuss the grave situation now advancing from the south.

Black Elk took his place of honor at the back of the tepee facing the opening, and the peace pipe was lit and smoked all around. All seven tribes of the Sioux believed that smoke from the peace pipe brought men's minds and thoughts into sharp focus and harmony. They believed that there was power and wisdom to be gained from the smoke and that the red stone ceremonial pipe was thought to make a man have visions that would assure victories over his future enemies.

When the pipe reached him, Long Rider took the hot bowl in his left hand and the stem in his right, then he raised the pipe to the spirits of the West, North, East, and South before he lowered it toward the earth and then to the sky. When he puffed the harsh willow bark, he closed his eyes and felt the weakness caused by his bullet wounds slip away from his body. He allowed his mind to drift with the smoke and when he opened his eyes, he felt good and certain that he would speak wisely to the people.

Gabe passed the pipe to the warrior on his left, and when it had gone completely around the circle, Black Elk set it down between his knees and was silent a long time before he said, "My brothers, things are very bad

for us now. You know that the iron horse is coming and
there are many soldiers led by the foolish Captain Stone
and the railroad man named Lydick. They will not turn
back this time but will hunt us into these mountains and
find our buffalo. They will kill us and force our women
and children to return to the reservation. They will shoot
all the buffalo.''

This said, Black Elk looked around the circle of grim-
faced men, warriors all tested in battle and found worthy
in strength, wisdom and courage. A warrior named Lone
Buffalo spoke first. ''I have seen many seasons and am
not afraid to die. I will fight the soldiers and kill them
like Red Cloud and Crazy Horse did to the soldiers of
Yellow Hair at the Little Big Horn.''

Gabe remained silent as another warrior voiced the
same opinion. ''I, Strong Horse, will fight as well. I will
never let the blue coats come into these mountains and
kill more buffalo.''

But a third warrior had a differing point of view. ''My
brothers, you know Iron Lance does not fear death. But
we must live so that the Sioux blood will not disappear
from the face of the earth. I say we should send Long
Rider forward to negotiate a peace. If it is good, then
we come down from these mountains and give ourselves
over to the soldiers.''

''That is no good!'' a big warrior named Spotted Horse
growled. ''If we give ourselves up, the soldiers will kill
our buffalo. We will be herded like sheep to the reservation and punished by starvation when the deep cold
strikes again. I say it is better to die like men than to
live like slaves!''

Other warriors joined in, each respectful and careful
to avoid argument among themselves. As far as Long
Rider could see, the council was about evenly split between attacking the soldiers outright, or trying to negotiate a good peace that would allow the Hunkpapa and
any other hostiles to remain free to roam and hunt as

long as they promised not to cause trouble.

At last, Long Rider was the only member of the war council who had not yet spoken. Black Elk said, "You may speak now and tell us what you would do."

Gabe closed his eyes for a moment and considered all that he had heard in this big tepee. He sincerely wished he could simply meet with Captain Stone and Aaron Lydick and make some kind of a fair deal. But in his heart, he knew that there was little chance of making peace at any price. The stakes for both the white men were too high. Lydick needed the buffalo meat and hides to make his damned northern spur railroad show a healthy profit.

"My brothers," Long Rider began, studying each man's face. "My heart aches for the people and I want to say that we can have a peace. But in truth, this cannot be as long as two men live. Those two men, Aaron Lydick and Captain Stone, are dishonorable and will betray us. They will make any promise that will serve their purpose, but their hearts are evil. This I know, for I have been in the Army stockades and have spoken with the railroad man and know his purpose is to wipe out every buffalo that yet lives on our plains."

Long Rider paused for a full minute to let his words sink into the minds of his friends, and then continued. "Because these words I know to be true, I must kill them to end this trouble. Without them, the soldiers will have no leader and they will return to Fort York. Before they could return to these mountains, it will be winter and the snows will be too deep."

His eyes came to rest on Black Elk and he finished his words by saying, "If I kill the railroad builder and the Army captain, then no one can say that it was done by the Indian, for I am a white man by blood. But if you and your warriors kill these same men, more soldiers will come and their revenge will be very bad against the

Hunkpapa and all the other Sioux people. That is why I must do the killing alone.''

Black Elk's lips tightened together and his eyes drifted around the circle of men. It was obvious to Long Rider that the leader of the Hunkpapa agreed with his reasoning but was very reluctant to set the plan in motion. ''This is all you have to say?''

''Yes.''

Black Elk nodded. ''My brothers, Long Rider has spoken well and though my heart is heavy in this talk, I say that he is right.''

''He will be shot or hanged by the whites,'' Cold Hand said, voicing everyone's silent thoughts.

Long Rider held his tongue for a moment, then carefully phrased his response. He was sure the council would not let him go alone if he offered no hope of living to himself. Yet he had to be honest without bragging of his fighting prowess. ''I have been in many fights,'' he said, looking at each man in the circle, ''just as have each of my brothers seated here in this council. And there have been times when I thought I would surely die. But every time, the Great Spirit gave me good fortune and great strength to live another day. I do not know how I will kill the railroad man and the bad Army captain. They have many guns around to protect them. I only know that it will happen. As for my own life, if I lose it in this way, it will be for a good reason. I would have no regrets, my brothers.''

The warriors were moved by Long Rider's strong but simply spoken words. He was not an eloquent man, not like the great chiefs, Sitting Bull, Red Cloud, and Crazy Horse. But when Long Rider spoke, it was good to listen.

Black Elk summed up everyone's feelings when he said. ''We will move our camp deeper into the mountains where the buffalo herd is hidden. As soon as you are strong enough, you will go to find the whites and kill their leaders. I ask only that you take one of us to follow you so that we will know when the leaders of our enemies are dead.''

It was a fair request and Long Rider nodded. "Already Cold Hand has faced death at my side and lived to kill his enemies, the Blackfeet. We will go together again.''

Cold Hand straightened with pride. He was probably the least well known among his peers but Long Rider had just bestowed upon him a great honor, one made even more significant given his recent bullet wound and brush with death.

All eyes turned to Cold Hand, who climbed to his feet and thumped his chest with his fist. "I will be ready to ride when you are ready.''

Long Rider climbed to his own feet. The meeting was ended. He had committed himself to killing both Aaron Lydick and Captain William Stone because they were ruthless and corrupt men who held great power and intended to use it against the People.

Gabe bowed to Black Elk and then went outside into the warm sun. He took a deep breath and headed for a nearby stream where he could wash before entering the Hunkpapa sweat lodge, where he would purify himself and cleanse away the last vestiges of his sickness.

It would take a day, possibly even two before he was strong enough to start riding south with Cold Hand to intercept the soldiers. Gabe wondered how many soldiers were coming. But did it really matter? Two hundred or four hundred, they would be strong enough to defeat this village and kill the buffalo for Aaron Lydick.

No, Gabe thought as he pulled off his shirt and slowly undressed to wade out into the cold, refreshing water. I will find a way to do what must be done, and then I will try to stay alive to fight another day if the Great Spirit wishes that to be.

That evening around the campfire, Long Rider enjoyed himself and spoke of many things to John Horner and Annie Rooney. He told them about his childhood and explained the Sioux ways and customs so that they would understand how to live among these people as long as they intended to stay. But it was not until he was about ready to leave that he told the young newlyweds that he was going to intercept Aaron Lydick and the United States cavalry troops headed north.

"You're insane!" the blacksmith blurted in astonishment. "Certainly that Wyatt Noonan fella will be at Lydick's side. And if he isn't the first one to kill you, then one of the soldiers will be."

Annie appeared to be equally amazed and upset. "It's true. You would be shot on sight."

"There is no choice," Long Rider told them. "If I can manage to kill Lydick and the captain, then the soldiers will become confused and lose their purpose. They will return to Fort York and messages will be sent to Washington. I know something about the Army. There will be an inquiry."

"And you'll be dead!" Annie cried.

Gabe would have loved to have taken the young woman in his arms and comforted her, but that, of course, was now entirely out of the question.

"I intend to figure out some way to survive this," he said. "I do not think my time has come to die."

"You're a fool, Conrad," the blacksmith said with a shake of his head. "Unless you can shoot them both from long distance and then outrun the whole bunch, I don't think you'll stand a chance. Them boys in blue sure as hell won't let you murder their commanding officer and live to face a trial."

"I know," Gabe said. "And if I still had Noonan's telescopic sight and hunting rifle, I'd have no hesitation in using it on both men. But Noonan took not only his own weapons back, but mine as well."

"So how are you going to kill him?"

"I don't know yet," Gabe admitted. "But I'll have a few days to think on it."

Protest rose in Annie's face but before she could think of any more arguments, Gabe said his good-bye and left. He walked swiftly through the dark camp and when he found his own tepee, he went inside and lay down on his buffalo robe, knowing that sleep would not come easily if he worried about how he intended to carry out the nearly impossible task he had given himself.

So instead, he thought of Holly Brown and imagined that he would live to make love to her someday. It was a nice thought and he fell asleep and dreamed of the woman all through the night.

CHAPTER FIFTEEN

Holly Brown knew that she had made a big mistake in coming to Summer Creek when she tried to start her newspaper only to find that there were no available stores to rent. Furthermore, when she talked to the banker, Mr. Adams, she learned that the bank would not be interested in lending her any money.

"I think," Mr. Adams said, his voice dripping with false regret, "that you had better go to Mr. Lydick and make your arrangements."

"I've been to him and I'd rather make my own arrangements."

"I'm afraid that is out of the question," the banker had said with sickly smile. "Good day, ma'am."

Holly had heard the snickers that accompanied her exit from the bank and her cheeks had turned crimson with embarrassment. But it was no better than she deserved. She'd fallen into Aaron's trap and now she was caught and all the squirming in the world would not get her free.

Holly desperately wanted to be free. She knew that she was never going to have any respect here in Summer Creek. Except for Edna Weaver, the respectable women treated her like dirt. Worse than dirt, since they would have nothing to do with her at all. So she went to see Aaron to ask him for a one-way ticket out of Summer Creek. She would ride the train to California if he'd give her enough money. And if he wouldn't, then she'd ride the train as far west as it would take her just so long as she got out of this town.

"Ah, my dear Miss Holly!" Aaron said when she knocked on his office door and was bid to enter. "You are just in time to renew your acquaintance with Captain Stone!"

Holly had no interest whatsoever in renewing her acquaintance with the arrogant and ruthless captain who'd kicked her out of Fort York. "Good day," she said stiffly.

"You are looking more beautiful than ever," Captain Stone said, his eyes lingering on her bosom. "I just knew that city life would suit you far better than doing laundry at Fort York. I think I did you a very large favor."

"Of course you do," she replied. "Your kind always thinks it knows what is best for others. But you can't see the forest for trees, and I have no interest in discussing my personal business with you."

Stone blushed with embarrassment but said nothing.

"My dear woman," Lydick said. "You seem very upset. Perhaps we need to talk at once."

"I'll say what I have to say right now," Holly blurted, deciding to plunge ahead with her request despite Captain Stone's presence. "There is a train leaving for California this afternoon and I'd like to be on it."

Lydick's expression had been one of concern at first; now he scowled. "You are free to do whatever you wish, but I think you are being impetuous and foolhardy."

Holly's lips turned down at the corners. "You share

the same dictatorial fantasies as your trained captain. Aaron, I need train fare out of here.''

Aaron paled and it was all he could do to whisper, ''And if I refuse to honor your request?''

''Then I'll pack a bag and walk,'' she said. ''I am leaving Summer Creek today. I'll go anywhere to get out of your town and go someplace where I can start over again. I'm finished with your high-handedness and tired of living in your little Wyoming fiefdom where no one will say what they think in fear of displeasing your highness.''

''You insult me, then expect money?'' Aaron turned to the captain and tried to force a laugh. ''Women. Will any of us ever understand them for a single minute?''

Stone had recovered his composure. ''No, I'm afraid not. It seems the more beautiful they are, the more acidic their dispositions.''

''I need the money now,'' Holly said. ''Our arrangement is finished.''

Aaron came out of his office chair. ''Is it really? Listen, why don't we discuss this as soon as the captain and I have finished a matter of utmost importance concerning a man you no doubt well remember.''

Despite herself, Holly asked, ''And who would that be?''

Aaron smiled coldly for she had taken his bait. ''The one that you went walking with the day you first arrived in Summer Creek. I believe he is the man that the Sioux called Long Rider.''

Holly blinked. She knew she was stepping right back into his trap but she could not help but ask, ''And what about him?''

''Well,'' Aaron said, ''the man was shot up near the Powder River. He may be dead, but then again he might well be alive. He was brought down south on a travois and was left with a woman named Annie Rooney. I'm afraid that her reputation is no more respectable than your own. She is sort of a . . . well, loose woman."

Holly stiffened. "Why are you telling me all this?"

Lydick steepled his fingers together. "Because," he said, "you just told me you would be happy to go anywhere. How about traveling north on my railroad with Captain Stone and I to join his soldiers and participate in a foray deep into Indian country?"

"Why in the world should I do that?"

"To earn a ticket to California, of course! And to allow me to show you off in the new finery I've bought you since you've been here."

Holly clenched her fists at her sides. "You want to shame me before the soldiers of Fort York, the very men my late husband knew and even led on patrol."

"Excuse me," Captain Stone said. "But unofficially, your late husband was a disgrace to his uniform. He was a drunk and a—"

Captain Stone did not have time to finish before Holly struck his cheek with a loud smacking sound. Her voice shook when she grated, "Stone, you are even worse. You'd sell your mother for a dollar and I know that you've cheated the Indians and broken every treaty that was ever made between those people and ours."

"Long Rider must have gotten between your pretty legs," Stone hissed. "Because he seeded you with his brand of poison."

Holly swung at him again but this time the captain caught her arm and twisted it violently. It caused her to cry out in pain and kick him in the shin. The captain paled, loosed her arm, and balled his fist.

"Enough!" Aaron shouted. "Captain Stone, do not disgrace yourself further by attacking a woman. We leave within the hour to join your men."

Stone's eyes smoldered with hatred but Holly did not give a damn. Stone turned on his heel and marched out the door, slamming it hard in his wake.

"My, my," Aaron said, clicking his tongue. "You

really know how to hit a man where it hurts, don't you.''

"I've learned a few things about life."

"Are you going to accept my offer?"

"Yes," she heard herself say.

"Good!" He came around the table, walked briskly to his door, and locked it.

"What are you doing that for?"

In answer, Aaron went over to his big leather couch and sat down. He patted the cushion beside him and said, "We only have an hour and I have some details yet to attend to, so hurry up and take off your clothes and get over here."

"I will not!"

He stood up and went to the door. "You can walk to California or ride in style to California and have enough money to buy respectability when you arrive. Make your choice this very instant."

Holly was trembling. "I hate you," she whispered. "And I don't trust you!"

He went to his desk and drew a little key from his vest pocket which he used to unlock his middle sliding drawer. Taking out a small stack of twenty-dollar bills, he counted out loud until the figure totaled five hundred dollars.

"It's yours right now," he said. "All you have to do is promise to come with me and do as I say from this moment until the moment we return with Long Rider's scalp tacked to a board. What is your answer? Be quick about making it, I'm out of patience and time."

Holly stared at the money. Five hundred dollars was more than she'd ever seen in one place and it could all be hers if she could endure this creature for another few weeks. He would insult her, treat her like a slave to make himself look grand and powerful, she knew that. He would use her shamelessly for his own pleasure and probably groan and carry on so loudly out on the campaign that the troops could not help but hear his pleasure.

That was his pound of flesh, and in return he would pay her enough money not only to reach California, but also to start a new life with money and respectability.

Holly walked over and snatched up the money. Aaron laughed and unbuckled his trousers. "Get it off," he snarled. "And get your sweet ass onto my leather couch."

Holly nodded. She felt so sick and disgusted that she wanted to kill him, and then herself. Instead, she quickly undressed and went to his couch, where he stood with a hard erection in his hand.

"Open wide," he said with a laugh as he climbed between her legs and violently slammed his manhood up into her, liking the way she gasped in pain because of her dryness.

He took her cruelly, like a stallion, or, more aptly, like a boar takes a sow. Holly clutched the five hundred dollars in her hand and tried to put herself somewhere far away. But it wasn't easy.

When he groaned and his hips jerked spasmodically to empty himself inside of her, Holly whimpered and beat at his back with the money still clutched in her white fists.

When the train reached the end of the line, Holly peered out the window to see the small army of laborers shouting and waving a staged greeting for their boss, Aaron Lydick. It was obvious to anyone that the laborers had been forced to make a big show of Aaron's arrival.

Obviously pleased by the reception, Aaron waved at the crowd, then pulled Holly to her feet and said, "Come, my dear. Your beauty is a source of some pride to me and I want you to wave to the men and pretend that you are very happy to be at my side when I address the laborers."

Holly was pulled into the aisle and felt herself being gently, but firmly, pushed toward the rear platform of the passenger car. Outside, the sun was shining and there was a strong breeze coming down from the north, followed by some dark storm clouds that hinted at a summer squall. About a hundred yards to the north, the United States Cavalry had bivouacked and Holly was astonished at their numbers. This was not simply a patrol, or even a company; the force that they were to join approached battalion strength.

"Gentlemen!" Aaron called, extending his arms outward in a gesture that asked for silence. "It is my understanding that you have been meeting your daily mileage goals, and I am very pleased with the work I see here."

He paused. "I am sure that some of you remember a man named Long Rider who came by. As it turns out, he is an Indian lover and a betrayer of the white man. He has most recently killed Mr. Purvis Monk, whom some of you knew as a friend."

No one said a word and Holly would have bet anything that Purvis Monk hadn't a friend in the world.

"At any rate, I am afraid that Long Rider has rejoined hostile Indians up near the Powder River. It is also predictable that Long Rider is stirring up trouble again. What we are going to do, under Captain Stone's command and military leadership, is to find Long Rider and the hostiles and either capture every last one of them, or kill them— the choice belongs to them."

The railroad workers roared with approval and several raised clenched fists and begged to be given rifles so that they might be allowed to share in the fun.

Lydick ignored their pleas and grinned broadly. "We also intend to bring back enough buffalo meat to have the damndest big celebration ever held in this part of the country. I will give you men the afternoon off—with pay—and have twenty kegs of beer hauled up so that we can blow off some steam and then put our backs to the important work ahead. If we put our backs to it, I believe we can reach the lower Powder River country before the first snows fall!''

More shouting, clapping. and hooting came from the workers.

Aaron shoved Holly forward and as they were ushered through the boisterous crowd, he yelled, ''So, men, let's build ourselves a railroad! And let's give a hand to Captain Stone and the Twenty-third Cavalry's fighting men, who are going to rid this country of the red man once and for all!''

The mob howled with delight and now there was no need for anyone to prompt them into shouting and cheering for Aaron Lydick. Holly was thrown up onto the back of a horse, and then Aaron swung up on his own animal and waved to the crowd.

''Wave, damn you!'' he hissed out of the corner of his mouth.

Holly waved and then they galloped north to join the long column of mounted soldiers heading out for the Powder River.

CHAPTER SIXTEEN

Long Rider and Cold Hand stood on a high rise of land that gave them a commanding view of the eastern slope of the Big Horn Mountains for at least ten miles.

"I can see them coming," Long Rider said in Sioux to his companion. "And there is no doubt in my mind that Captain Stone will lead his cavalry through the canyon right below us. Once they enter and ride to this point, you pry loose that huge boulder to start a landslide and cut off their retreat."

Long Rider pointed to a scree of boulders down below. "I'll be down there, hidden from view. When the rockslide begins, there will be a lot of confusion. I'll step out and try to kill both Stone and Lydick. If I fail, I'll try to get out of there alive and meet you back up here after dark. I can try again in the next day or two."

Cold Hand was not happy with the plan. "Even if you kill them, the soldiers will shoot you before you can get away. I do not like this."

"Me, neither," Long Rider said. "But it's the best one I can think of at the moment."

"If we had a buffalo rifle it would be better. We could use the long rifle to shoot them dead from up here."

"No," Long Rider said. "I'd get off the first shot but never a second before Lydick and Stone would be surrounded by soldiers protecting them. Both men have to be killed because they're in this thing together all the way."

Long Rider watched the approaching column and tried to hide the worry he felt building inside. He wasn't concerned about his own life, but about the destruction that this large a military force could do to the Hunkpapa and other free-roaming Indians as they continued toward Montana. Their numbers were too great to fight, and with leaders as ruthless as Aaron Lydick and Captain Stone, there would be pillage and slaughter in the Indian villages to the north.

"Go take your place beside the great boulder that will fall, my brother," Gabe said. "It is time that I go also."

Cold Hand left without another word and Long Rider watched him move swiftly through the pine trees. When the moment came, Gabe knew that Cold Hand would not fail to bring the huge boulder crashing down behind the soldiers, cutting off their retreat and creating momentary panic and disorder.

Gabe had an old black-powder Navy Colt pistol that Black Elk had given him as well as a muzzle-loading rifle that had seen better days. He had fired each weapon at least a dozen times to make sure he knew how it shot and what its individual shortcomings might be. The pistol shot high and tended to jam while the rifle was without sights but shot reasonably straight. It was Gabe's intention to first kill Captain Stone using the single-shot rifle, and then to draw his pistol and open fire on Lydick. If he could down them both, then he did not greatly care what happened to himself afterward. He'd try to escape, but not before he was dead certain that he'd accomplished the job he'd set out to do.

He reached the bottom of the narrow gap and spent five minutes searching for precisely the best firing position. When he found it, he hunkered down to wait.

An hour passed and sweat trickled continuously down Gabe's spine. His shoulder wound pained him and the sun beat down on the rocks to fill the narrow gap until the air shimmered with heat waves. A lizard inched its way across the rock to stare with blue, unblinking eyes at the motionless Long Rider. Somewhere off to the north, thunder drummed across the steaming plains, and dark clouds rolled south.

Gabe thought of many things and he made his peace with the Great Spirit, thanking him for the good things that he had known in this lifetime and being careful not to think of the bad things that had also been his lot.

At last, he heard the muffled sound of the approaching cavalry and eased the old rifle up onto the rock which would serve as a firing rest. The canyon was only about a half mile wide, but when the first horses suddenly appeared, Gabe took a sharp intake of breath to see that Holly Brown was riding directly between Lydick and the captain.

What the devil was she doing up in this country? Gabe's eyes lifted to the huge boulder that would soon begin to bounce down the canyon side and create havoc among the soldiers and their mounts. He dried his sweaty palms on his shirtsleeves, cocked the rifle, and waited for the party to begin.

He only had a moment to wait. The huge boulder rocked almost imperceptibly and a trickle of pebbles began to fall down on the soldiers below. Gabe saw a number of them look upward and then, suddenly, the boulder broke free of its mooring, appeared to hang still for a moment, and then came crashing downward, bringing a landslide of loose shale in its wake and filling the entrance to the narrow canyon.

When the boulder struck the far side of the canyon, Gabe felt the rocks around him tremble. He pressed his cheek to the stock of the muzzle-loader and drew a bead on the captain. He was squeezing the trigger when the man's horse whirled in fear. The muzzle-loader bellowed with white smoke and flame, but even as the heavy lead ball it hurled was launched, Gabe knew that he'd missed. The horse had saved its rider and now, Aaron Lydick was grabbing Holly and throwing himself off his mount and diving for cover.

Gabe swore in futility as his six-gun bucked twice, but the dust was already so thick that he had nothing clear to aim for, not even the captain, who disappeared to the rear in a desperate attempt to put himself out of harm's way.

Long Rider gave himself two minutes before order was restored and the soldiers had him in their sights' and began their fire. Realizing that he had failed, he was determined to have another chance, so he left the old rifle and began to climb in his moccasins. He moved like a mountain lion toward the rim despite the problems created by his injured shoulder and the fact that his strength was not yet fully recovered.

"Get him!" Lydick shouted. "There, up on the rocks!"

Gabe was better than halfway up when the first shot screamed off a nearby boulder. He kept moving, his chest heaving and the hard muscles of his long legs beginning to burn. The bullets began to spray the rocks all around him, but still he climbed until he heard the powerful blast of Lydick's hunting rifle and felt shards of granite bury themselves in his cheek and forehead. He knew that in three seconds or less he would again be in the cross hairs of Lydick's rifle, and this time he would be shot through the chest.

Long Rider dived for cover among the rocks. To have attempted to make the last forty yards would have been suicidal. As if to emphasize this fact, the heavy bang of Lydick's rifle again overpowered the sharper explosions of the soldiers' carbines. Gabe was forced to press his body down into a crevasse in the rocks as dozens of slugs searched for him.

"Hold your fire!"

It was Captain Stone's voice and Long Rider waited, unable to predict what might happen next.

"Long Rider! Come down and give yourself up!"

It was Aaron Lydick who was shouting from down below. "Come down or Captain Stone will send his soldiers up to finish you off. You can't win this one!"

Gabe eased his head up and peered down into the canyon to see Lydick, the woman, and the Army captain, who was ordering twenty men to dismount and prepare to assault the canyon side and take Long Rider by force. Gabe could tell that the twenty soldiers chosen were reluctant to obey the order knowing that many of them would die before the sharpshooter above finally ran out of bullets or time.

Long Rider's fight was not with the soldiers who were now being forced to carry out their orders. Gabe had enough powder, caps, and balls to fire at least twenty rounds, though he doubted he'd be given that much time. Most likely, the many soldiers down below would keep up a steady volley and he'd be pinned down tighter than a tick on a dog.

Hell, he thought, the game is lost. Why kill a bunch of enlisted men? "All right," he yelled, "I'm coming down!"

"Throw out your gun and put your hands high in the air!" Captain Stone shouted.

Gabe tossed the old Navy Colt out and watched it sail end over end before it clattered to rocks below.

"Now the rifle!"

"I left it down below. It's a single-shot muzzle-loader."

"Sergeant, go check and see if he's lying or not," Stone commanded.

A moment later, the sergeant yelled, "I got it in my hands."

Satisfied, Stone yelled, "Come on out with your hands up high, Indian lover."

Gabe half expected to be gunned down the moment he exposed himself to fire, but there was no alternative, so he raised his hands and stood erect.

"Now come on down!"

Gabe obeyed for the sole reason that there were about two hundred rifles pointed at him from down below.

When he reached the floor of the canyon, Holly tried to rush to his side but Lydick grabbed her arm and twisted her to the ground. Gabe jumped for the man but Wyatt Noonan swung the butt of his Winchester rifle at the side of Gabe's head, bringing him down hard. Noonan stepped in and kicked Gabe in the side with the toe of his boot and would have done it a second time, but Holly screamed, "Get that animal away from him!"

"That's enough!" Lydick shouted. "I want him alive!"

"But he killed Purvis!"

"A man you loathed. Now, leave him alone."

Lydick squatted down beside Long Rider, who tried to clear what felt like a busted head. The railroad man grabbed him by the hair and pulled his chin up to hiss, "I'm going to give you one last chance to get smart. Now, either lead us to the Indians and their hidden buffalo herds, or say your prayers."

"All . . . all right," Long Rider choked.

Captain Stone was outraged. "Do you mean to tell me you're going to trust him again!"

"No," Lydick said, "but in chains and with two hundred soldiers around to watch him day and night, what do I have to lose by giving him the chance to save his hide and save us a fortune?''

"Not a damn thing, I guess.'' The captain did not sound pleased.

"You guessed right,'' Lydick said. "Get him on his feet and get him shackled. We can still cover a few miles before dark. Long Rider, how far is the nearest Indian village?''

"Two days' ride to the north.''

"How many Indians were up on the rim of this canyon helping you?''

"Just one.'' Long Rider grinned through his pain. "And he'll be on his way back to warn the others.''

"Damn!'' Captain Stone swore. "He's right! By the time we get there, every Indian in our path will be alerted and scattering for only God knows where.''

"The hell with the Indians this time,'' Lydick growled. "If we catch 'em, fine. But what I really want is their buffalo.''

Again, he grabbed Long Rider by the hair and wrenched his head back to stare piteously at his face, bloodied by the rock shards. "How far to their herd?''

"Seventy, maybe eighty miles.''

"They'd better be,'' Lydick whispered so that only Long Rider could hear. "Or you and Holly will be pushing up mountain daisies together next spring. Savvy?''

Gabe savvied, all right. Now he knew why Holly Brown was here and what would happen to her if he didn't find this ruthless son of a bitch a herd of buffalo.

CHAPTER SEVENTEEN

Long Rider was not a man who believed in giving up but he couldn't remember when things looked worse than now. His wrists were shackled behind his back and his legs were tied underneath his horse during the daytime so he couldn't even throw himself off his gelding down some rocky gorge. And now, at nighttime, when the camp lay sleeping, there were two sentries assigned to watch over him despite the fact that his arms and legs were shackled around a damn pine tree. One thing was painfully obvious—Aaron and Captain Stone were taking no chances.

Long Rider leaned his forehead against the bark of the tree and wished for sleep though he knew he would get none. This was his second wakeful night and tomorrow they were supposed to find the buffalo herd he'd promised. But they wouldn't. He'd led the Army about as far from the herds that Black Elk had told him about as was humanly possible. By tomorrow evening, Lydick and

Captain Stone would fabricate some reason to have him shot, of course, and while he was doing it, he'd have Holly shot as well.

Long Rider twisted his head around and noticed that the two privates who were supposed to be guarding him were sitting off a little ways, talking in low voices. They weren't paying him any attention, but why should they be, given the fact that he was bound hand and foot? Once more, Long Rider struggled to pull his wrists loose, knowing that it was no good. He'd worked them raw already and they were badly swollen, making escape even more unlikely.

Suddenly, Long Rider saw the faintest of shadows moving toward the guards. Long Rider blinked, not sure if his eyes were betraying him. Then, as if from out of the ground, Cold Hand sprang on both men with a knife. The Indian's blade flashed twice in the moonlight and Gabe heard each of the guards grunt as they toppled forward. A moment later, Cold Hand was at his side, whispering for the keys that would release his shackles.

"Captain Stone has them," Long Rider whispered. "He won't let anyone but himself touch the locks."

Cold Hand twisted around to stare at the huge encampment. There were other guards out at the perimeter of the camp, but he had slipped past them as silent as a ghost. "Which one is he?"

Long Rider didn't have to look. "He's the man in the tent."

"There are *two* tents."

Gabe pressed his forehead against the bark. "I forgot," he said, raging at himself because his mind was not thinking clearly for lack of sleep and the blow that Noonan had delivered with his own Winchester rifle. "I don't know which one."

"I will find him and his keys."

Gabe cursed at his helplessness as Cold Hand left his side and moved swiftly at a low crouch toward the tents.

By twisting his head and shoulders sideways, Gabe could see the Hunkpapa but it amazed him how he really had to look for him as he crept between the hundreds of sleeping soldiers. Gabe saw Cold Hand drop to the ground as Captain Stone's personal guard came walking around the tent. But when the man passed within two yards of the Indian, Cold Hand rose up and leaped on his back, his left hand clamping over the guard's mouth, his right hand driving the blade of his knife into the man's chest as his weight brought the soldier to rest.

Cold Hand eased into the tent. The next few minutes seemed like an eternity to Long Rider and he thought he heard a muffled cry before Cold Hand appeared in the faint moonlight with a knife in one hand and keys in the other. The Indian stood frozen for almost a full minute before he lowered himself to the ground and came slithering back through the camp. Minutes later, Long Rider was free.

"Is Captain Stone dead?"

Cold Hand nodded with satisfaction. He reached into a leather pouch he had tied to his belt and handed Gabe the officer's pistol and then yanked Stone's bloody scalp out to hold it up in the moonlight. "That one will never order soldiers to kill our buffalo."

The Sioux returned his grisly trophy to his pouch and said, "Come, Long Rider, I have our horses waiting."

"There is a woman," Gabe said, touching his savior's arm. "I have to bring her or she will be killed. I need three horses."

Most men would have objected, given the circumstances, but not this one. "I will meet you by the little stream that flows to the wide river," Cold Hand said.

"I will be there soon, my brother." Gabe took the gun but wished for a knife instead. To fire a gun would be to alert the entire camp, and that would prove fatal.

He was so stiff and weak that it took him three times longer than it had taken Cold Hand to sneak back to the tent. Long Rider peered through the flap of the captain's tent to see him lying facedown. Gabe felt no regrets at all for Captain Stone. The man was no good.

He moved quickly to Lydick's tent. Long Rider would have given almost anything to be able to strike a match but that, of course, was entirely out of the question. He entered the tent and stood for a long moment, looking at two Army cots and wondering which one Holly was sleeping in.

Both she and Lydick were buried under the blankets so Long Rider, with his gun in his right hand, gently slipped his left hand under the covers and when his fingers touched a soft, mounded breast, he knew that he'd found Holly.

"Not again," she moaned. "Get away from me!"

Lydick stirred but did not awaken. Gabe held his breath and then pulled his hand back and placed it over Holly's mouth, clamping it down tight. He felt her stiffen under him and he pressed his lips to her ear. "It's Long Rider! We're getting out of here!"

Holly did not have to be told twice. She was up and throwing herself into his arms, hugging his neck and kissing his bloodied face. Gabe had to practically tear her away from him. He took her hand and was about to step outside when he remembered that Lydick could not be allowed to live to destroy the Indians and their buffalo and then to financially ruin a bunch of poor homesteaders.

"Go outside and wait for me a moment, Holly. I have something to do before I go."

"Do you—"

"You know that I do," he said. "But I can't kill a man in his sleep."

A voice from outside the tent said, "You won't have to, Long Rider, 'cause I'm going to kill you first!"

Gabe threw his arm out and knocked Holly sideways as his gun came up. Even if he'd had the time to consider the disastrous consequences of firing in the middle of an

Army camp he'd still have pulled the trigger. Noonan's hand was already filled with iron and yet it was so dark in the tent that the gunfighter did not have a good silhouette target. So as Holly fell one way and Gabe threw his body to the other side, Noonan unleashed two bullets before Gabe pulled the trigger of his Army revolver.

Noonan missed Long Rider and his slugs hit Aaron Lydick twice in the body. Gabe's bullet struck the gunfighter right in the breastbone and drove him back a step. A second bullet crashed through the tent opening, and Wyatt Noonan took it in the forehead and stiffened on his heels before he went over backward.

Gabe and Holly ran for their lives. They could hear shouts and curses, and when they came to the meeting place where Cold Hand held their waiting horses, Gabe started to throw Holly onto the back of a waiting horse but she resisted.

"What's wrong with you?"

"It was Wyatt Noonan that killed Aaron, not you! If I run away with you now, you'll be hunted down for murder."

"Get on the horse! I killed Noonan, remember. Cold Hand killed and scalped Captain Stone and had to kill a couple of guards as well. It's done!"

But Holly backed away. "No," she said defiantly. "I will go before a military court and expose everything those men tried to do, and I'll testify that you didn't kill either one of them."

"They won't believe you!"

"Oh yes, they will. I know where Aaron's records are. I know where he keeps his pay-off accounts and most of all, I know the Army doesn't want the newspapers to know that some of its highest officers were taking bribes from Aaron Lydick. I know what I'm doing so get out of here while you can!"

Long Rider heard the sound of boots striking the hard ground and he knew that the soldiers would soon find them. He mounted his horse. "Are you sure?"

"The Army ruined my husband and I owe it a black eye. As for Aaron . . . well, I know where he keeps a bundle of money hidden that I think I've earned."

"Will I see you again?"

"No," she said. "Not unless you come to California and find me someplace living in a big house by the sea."

"I'll find you someday," Long Rider promised as he wheeled his horse around. "Give 'em hell, Holly!"

"Long Rider!" she yelled into the night. "You can just bet on it!"